Dementor

Headmaster's tower

Hungarian Horntail

Great Hall

LEGO Harry Potter

MAGICAL TREASURY

A VISUAL GUIDE TO THE WIZARDING WORLD

Evergreen trees surround the castle

Written by
Elizabeth Dowsett

Contents

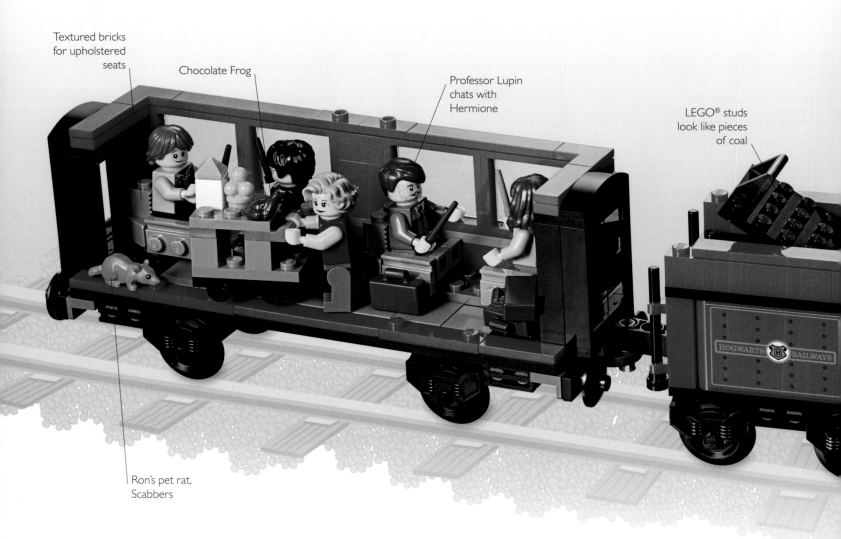

Textured bricks for upholstered seats

Chocolate Frog

Professor Lupin chats with Hermione

LEGO® studs look like pieces of coal

HOGWARTS RAILWAYS

Ron's pet rat, Scabbers

Handrails

Driver's cab with controls and fire

Connecting rod on drive wheels moves as train goes forward

5972

HOGWARTS CASTLE

Introduction

Within our world there exists another world—a magical place that sits alongside our everyday lives, and you don't have to walk through a brick wall to find it. It's a place where one of the most popular toys combines with one of the biggest movie franchises to create something new and spectacular. It's the world of LEGO® Harry Potter™ and Fantastic Beasts™.

Delve into the pages of this book (which thankfully has no monstrous, snapping pages) to discover how this spellbinding world has been re-created in LEGO sets since 2018. These minifigures study magic, play Quidditch, and battle Dark forces. They live in incredible buildings, ride fantastical vehicles, and care for amazing creatures. Everything is brought to life, not with charms or transfiguration, but with the ingenious skills of LEGO designers and the versatility of LEGO bricks. See custom-made pieces like the tiny Golden Snitch and marvel at clever new uses for classic LEGO pieces. A LEGO frog in brown looks like a delicious chocolate treat and a ski pole turned upside down makes a perfect spire for one of Hogwarts' many towers.

Get ready to enter into this wonderful, brick-built world of witches and wizards.

Ford Anglia crashed in tree

Hinged suitcases can be opened

Whomping Willow

Data files

Throughout the book, you can find all the key details of each LEGO Harry Potter and Fantastic Beasts set shown. A data file gives each set's official name, the year of its first release, its LEGO identification number, the number of LEGO pieces—or elements—in it, and the number of minifigures in it.

Set name The Knight Bus
Year 2019
Set number 75957
Pieces 403
Minifigures 3

Feather floats thanks to Hermione's *Wingardium Leviosa* spell

Harry's owl, Hedwig

Caretaker Filch patrols at night

Magical Students

Harry Potter

Wild, unruly hair

Lightning-bolt scar

Muggle (non-wizard) clothes

Short, nonposable legs

Harry Potter has had a very miserable life growing up with his mean Aunt Petunia and Uncle Vernon and their bully of a son, Dudley. Harry believes that he is nothing special. But then, on his 11th birthday, everything changes. Harry finds out that not only is there a wizarding world full of magic, but that he is actually a wizard himself. In fact, he's a very famous one.

The Boy Who Lived

All Harry's minifigures have his distinctive round glasses and the lightning-bolt-shaped scar on his forehead. Harry is famous among wizards because he survived an attack from a Dark wizard called Voldemort when he was only a baby. Harry's parents were killed, but his only injury was the scar.

Cauldron piece with a metallic finish

Set name Harry's Journey to Hogwarts
Year 2018
Set number 30407
Pieces 40
Minifigures 1

Luggage cart

Off to school

Harry receives an acceptance letter from Hogwarts School of Witchcraft and Wizardry—even though he's never heard of it! He's all packed up for his journey to school in this small set. It comes with all the supplies he needs, such as a pewter cauldron and a wand.

Second year

Casual open shirt

Suitcase with supplies for school

Harry sets off for his second year at school in Muggle clothes—a red checked shirt and gray trousers. After missing the Hogwarts Express, he and Ron Weasley travel to school in Mr. Weasley's blue flying Ford Anglia car. This Harry minifigure appears with Ron and the magical car in Hogwarts Whomping Willow (set 75953).

Third year

In tan trousers and a dark-blue jacket, Harry's minifigure appears in three LEGO® sets based on his third-year adventures. He battles Dementors in Expecto Patronum (set 75945), helps save a Hippogriff in Hagrid's Hut: Buckbeak's Rescue (set 75947), and takes a bumpy ride on The Knight Bus (set 75957).

Chocolate snack to eat on the Knight Bus

Hedwig

Hogwarts students are allowed to bring an owl, a cat, or a toad to school. Harry's snowy owl is named Hedwig and was bought from Eeylops Owl Emporium. She travels safely in a cage built from LEGO telescope pieces in Harry's Journey to Hogwarts (set 30407). The cage has a LEGO clip for hanging it up.

Brick facts

In 2018, the LEGO Group introduced a new medium-height leg piece for young minifigures. It's shorter than regular legs but is still hinged, unlike the regular short, nonposable leg piece.

Longer hair sweeps across face

Knee-length robes

Hedwig is the only owl with this printing

Fourth year

In Harry's fourth year, both his minifigure and his hair have grown! The print for his Gryffindor robe continues onto his medium-sized leg pieces. This version of Harry is one of the 22 characters found in the LEGO® Harry Potter™ Minifigure Series, and is joined by his loyal friend Hedwig.

Privet Drive

For as long as Harry can remember, home has always been his aunt and uncle's house, but it's not a happy place. Aunt Petunia and Uncle Vernon reluctantly took Harry in when his parents died, and they never made Harry feel welcome. This suburban house may not look very exciting, but it has helped keep Harry safe and hidden from Dark magical forces for many years.

Set name 4 Privet Drive
Year 2020
Set number 75968
Pieces 797
Minifigures 6

Number 4

Mr. and Mrs. Dursley are very proud of their neat and tidy house in the Surrey town of Little Whinging. The LEGO set has a hinged side door for accessing the space under the stairs, where Harry is forced to sleep as a child. The main room has a shooting function that fires letters out of the fireplace.

Owl piece with outstretched wings

Barred window

Mr. Weasley's flying car "borrowed" by Ron

7990 TD

Ron pulls off Harry's bedroom window when he comes to collect him

Brick facts

A unique LEGO sign for Privet Drive stands on two jumper plates. It also has a stud for an owl or a cat to sit on while they watch events in the street.

PRIVET DRIVE

Magical Hogwarts letters unable to get through the nailed-up mail slot

Quidditch star

Harry soon discovers Quidditch, a game played on broomsticks. It turns out that he's very good at it and he plays for his house, Gryffindor, as their youngest Seeker in a century. His minifigure wears the team's scarlet-and-gold robes and bright-white trousers—which won't stay white for long on a muddy pitch!

Warm, ribbed sweater under robes

Gryffindor crest

Leather flying gloves

Brick facts

You can't play Quidditch without a broomstick. Harry has a Nimbus 2000 and later a Firebolt. His brown LEGO broom is a single piece that was originally designed for the LEGO® Fabuland™ theme.

Brick-built Triwizard Cup

Magical blue fire burns in cup

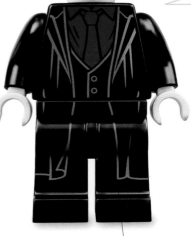

Short, neat haircut

Slug Clubber

During Harry's sixth year, he is invited to be part of Professor Slughorn's exclusive Slug Club—a collection of the professor's favorite students. At a Slug Club party in Hogwarts Astronomy Tower (set 75969), Harry wears his best black wizarding robes. Harry is a reluctant guest, because he doesn't like special attention.

Formal dress robes extend to full-size legs

Triwizard champion

The winner of the Triwizard Tournament wins eternal glory, but also money and this Triwizard Cup. To his shock, Harry is selected to take part in the contest. For one of the tournament's three tasks, he wears Gryffindor red but also a crest with all four houses. He is competing for the whole of Hogwarts, after all!

Ron Weasley

Ron comes from a big, boisterous family. He meets Harry at King's Cross station on the first day of school and they become best friends. Sometimes Ron feels second best compared to his older brothers or his famous friend, but he proves himself to be a worthy Gryffindor: strong, courageous, and loyal. These qualities help him on many dangerous adventures.

Red hair is a Weasley family trait

Freckles

Checked jacket

Brave adventurer

Ron follows in his five older brothers' footsteps when he sets off for school on his short LEGO legs in Hogwarts Express (set 75955). The same brave minifigure carries a lantern to light his way when he ventures into the Forbidden Forest in Aragog's Lair (set 75950).

Chess master

Every Christmas Ron gets a personalized hand-knitted sweater from his mom, featuring an "R" for Ron. This cozy sweater makes a comfy outfit for a game of wizard chess during the school holidays. Both Ron and the mini game come with the 2019 LEGO Harry Potter Advent Calendar (set 75964).

Model Gryffindor

Like all his brothers before him, Ron is sorted into Gryffindor house. Settling into school in Hogwarts Great Hall (set 75954), young Ron has short legs and a neatly pressed red-and-gold Gryffindor uniform, which could have been worn by one of his brothers before him.

Short, nonposable legs

Brick facts

Two double-sided panels come with the Mirror of Erised. The reflections can be swapped depending on who looks in the mirror. Ron sees himself as Head Boy and Quidditch Captain.

House Cup

Runaway Ron

Having missed the Hogwarts Express in their second year, Ron and Harry set off for school in Mr. Weasley's flying car—a blue Ford Anglia. The boys make it to Hogwarts, but crash-land in the Whomping Willow. They're stuck there until the tree violently shakes them out.

Bare, gnarly branches hold car in place

Bald patch printed on Scabbers' head

Rat keeper

Ron's pet rat, Scabbers, joins him at Hogwarts and in the LEGO Harry Potter Minifigure Series. Ron looks a little older now he is in his third year. He also has a unique torso— because no one else has such a bedraggled uniform.

Untidy uniform

Secret entrance to a tunnel beneath the tree

Set name Hogwarts Whomping Willow
Year 2018
Set number 75953
Pieces 753
Minifigures 6

Hair is longer in the fourth year

Frilly dress robes

Casual collared t-shirt

Behind the times

Poor Ron does not enjoy the Yule Ball. Hermione is going with Viktor Krum and, to make matters worse, Ron is in old-fashioned robes that his mom sent him. In Ron's own words, they make him look like his Great-Aunt Tessie!

Won Won

Now in his sixth year at Hogwarts, Ron has full-size minifigure legs. In Hogwarts Astronomy Tower (set 75969), Ron explores the castle with Lavender Brown. The pair exchange presents, and romance blossoms between Lavender and her love, "Won Won."

Set name Attack on the Burrow
Year 2020
Set number 75980
Pieces 1,047
Minifigures 8

Roof terrace for minifigures

Roof patched up in different shades

Wooden planks show regular repairs

Wooden frame is a remnant of the original Tudor dwelling

Upper floors are supported at an angle on hinged bricks

Ancient stained-glass window

Front section hinges open to reveal fireplace

Pig pen

The Burrow

The Weasleys don't have the latest fashions and gadgets, but they do have a cozy place to live. The crooked but much-loved Burrow is a welcome second home for Harry. Filled with chatter, laughter, and wizarding wonders, it couldn't be more different from Privet Drive. But Harry puts it at risk when he stays, drawing the fire of some sinister witches and wizards.

Hodgepodge house

Located near the Devon village of Ottery St. Catchpole, The Burrow looks like a physical impossibility. It is probably held up with magic as much as with nails and cement! The house grew as the family did, with extra rooms piled on the top. This LEGO model captures its higgledy-piggledy style over four crooked floors.

Ron's bedroom

During the school holidays, Ron writes letters for Pigwidgeon to carry to Harry—when Harry isn't staying at The Burrow, that is! Ron has decorated his room with a Chudley Cannons poster, and his bedding is the same bright orange as the Quidditch team's robes.

Floo in the fire

The Burrow is connected to the Floo Network—a transportation grid along which people can be transported using magic powder. Entrances to the network are fireplaces, and this LEGO one has a mechanism to change orange flames to green as the floo powder burns.

Molly Weasley

Proud mother hen of the Weasley clan, Molly bustles about The Burrow looking after everyone. With an intricately knitted cardigan and sloped-brick skirt, her minifigure has a crinkly, friendly face. In Harry's second year, Molly teaches him how to use magical green powder to travel on the Floo Network.

Floo powder

Arthur Weasley

A warm, kind wizard, Arthur Weasley works for the Misuse of Muggle Artifacts Office at the Ministry of Magic. He's fascinated by all things Muggle. Much of The Burrow's clutter is made up of items he's brought home to figure out how they work. He marvels at their magic-free technology.

Open and cheerful expression

Frayed patchwork cardigan

Rear view

Clipped-back hair

Ginny Weasley

Only one of Ron's six siblings is at home in this set. Ron's younger (and only) sister, Ginny, appears in casual trousers and a top for a relaxing day at home during the holidays. She drinks tea in her bedroom on the first floor and goes outside to feed the pig in the sty.

Ginny's first minifigure has full-size legs

Heart of the home

The kitchen, where Molly Weasley prepares enormous meals with the help of magic, fills most of the ground floor. In pride of place is a grandfather-style clock. Instead of the time, the clock indicates the location of each member of the family—or if they're in mortal danger.

Hermione Granger

The brightest witch of her age, Hermione is very clever. She excels in her studies, but she's also good at using what she's learned in practical situations. Her knowledge has saved the day many times. Hermione is also a close and loyal friend to Harry and Ron—and not just because she keeps saving their lives!

Gryffindor tie

Comfy striped sweater has a hood printed on the back

Young Hermione's hair piece has bangs

Model student

Alert and ready to learn, first-year Hermione is in her Gryffindor school uniform with short, black legs. Hermione's parents are Muggles so she's new to magic, but she's read all about her new magical school in a book called *Hogwarts: A History*.

Muggle wear

In Hogwarts Express (set 75955), Hermione is in casual Muggle clothes so she doesn't draw any attention at King's Cross station. Students usually change into their uniforms once they're on board the school train.

Christmas countdown

It can get very cold at Hogwarts in winter. Hermione is wrapped up in a cozy Gryffindor scarf to admire the festive decorations in the LEGO Harry Potter Advent Calendar (set 75964). Most students go home for the holidays, but Hermione stays to keep Harry company—and spend extra time in the library.

LEGO star tops tree

Snowy tree is built around single bricks with four side studs threaded on a pole

Set name LEGO Harry Potter Advent Calendar

Year 2019

Set number 75964

Pieces 305

Minifigures 7

Top of the class

In the LEGO Harry Potter Minifigure series, Hermione's minifigure has a more grown-up face print and a sleeker hairstyle with no bangs. She wears a long, maroon-lined robe over her Gryffindor uniform and is accompanied by her orange cat, Crookshanks.

Robe worn over sweater and shirt

Time-Turner worn around neck

Time traveler

The only schoolwork Hermione struggles with is choosing which subjects to drop. Professor McGonagall gives her a Time-Turner so she can be in two lessons at once by repeating time. In Hagrid's Hut: Buckbeak's Rescue (set 75947), Hermione uses it to change events and save a Hippogriff.

Crookshanks is the only cat of this color using this LEGO mold

Practice makes perfect

Sixth-year Hermione's minifigure has straighter hair than when she was younger. She's learning to stand on her own two (full-size minifigure) legs in the face of great danger. Her serious expression is focused on practicing Defense Against the Dark Arts as part of a secret club, Dumbledore's Army, in Hogwarts Room of Requirement (set 75966).

Hogwarts cardigan worn for the first time

Brick facts

Patronuses are defensive charms that take a shimmering animal appearance. Hermione's is an otter. Its semi-solid form is captured in a transparent blue, glittery LEGO piece.

Platform 9¾

All aboard the Hogwarts Express! Every first of September this gleaming steam train leaves London's King's Cross station to take students to Hogwarts for the new school year. This LEGO set includes a section of the station with platforms 9, 10, the mysterious platform 9¾, and the famous scarlet locomotive.

Luggage car

Between the train's engine and the passenger car is a linked coal car. The plate is hinged so it can be lifted up, revealing lots of space for students' luggage—or a place for a minifigure to hide from the Dementor that comes with the set.

Wall and roof attach using just a few studs, so they can be easily removed for play

Windows open and close

Stairs cross over train tracks

Practical apron over patterned blouse

Trolley witch

This kind, elderly witch has been selling food and drinks on the Hogwarts Express for many years. Generations of students have looked forward to the rattle of her snack cart coming along the carriage. Her minifigure has wrinkles on her face and neatly coiffed hair.

Honeydukes Express

The Hogwarts Express gets students to school, but it's the Honeydukes Express snack cart that fills their stomachs and satisfies their sweet tooth. It's stocked with candy, ice cream, drinks, and even a Chocolate Frog—just make sure it doesn't jump out of the open window!

Platform 9¾

Ask a Muggle for directions to Platform 9¾ and they'll think you're trying to be funny. This secret platform is invisible to Muggles. To them, its entrance just looks like a solid brick wall located between the ordinary platforms 9 and 10. But that is where you'll find the Hogwarts Express. This special LEGO train has three sections: the distinctive red locomotive, a luggage or coal car, and a passenger carriage with seats for four minifigures.

Secret entrance

Wizards and witches walk straight at a section of brick wall to pass through to the magical platform. Minifigures access it thanks to two LEGO® Technic pins that allow the wall to swing. Ron pushes a cart loaded with his luggage and pet rat, Scabbers, ahead of him.

Solid wall swings up to allow Ron to pass through

Wanted poster shows Sirius Black

Set name Hogwarts Express
Year 2018
Set number 75955
Pieces 801
Minifigures 6

Brick facts

A specially printed 4x4 radar dish sits at the front of the train. It is printed with "5972" because the design of the train is based on the Great Western Railway 5972 Olton Hall steam train.

First minifigure with a Hogwarts sweater vest

Hogwarts students

Harry, Ron, and Hermione aren't the only young wizards and witches at Hogwarts. During the course of his studies, Harry finds a number of other friends—and an enemy— among his fellow students. Many of these classmates can be found in the LEGO Harry Potter Minifigure Series and come with their own special accessories.

Patronus charm protects against Dementors

Luna Lovegood

Dreamy Luna always expresses her own style, even in her Ravenclaw uniform. Luna believes she's protected from Nargles—mischievous magical creatures—by her Butterbeer cork necklace. She conjures another defensive aid, a blue Patronus in the form of a rabbit, in Hogwarts Room of Requirement (set 75966).

Cho Chang

Cho Chang is the first minifigure to appear wearing the Ravenclaw house tie. Her uniform also includes a special LEGO piece—a fabric skirt, similar to previous minifigures' capes. It's held between her torso and leg pieces. Fellow Ravenclaw Luna Lovegood wears the same piece in a colorful, non-uniform pattern in the LEGO Harry Potter Minifigure Series.

Owl clips onto minifigure hand

Skirt folds all the way around legs

Neville Longbottom

Neville needn't look so concerned. He's a whizz at Herbology, so isn't going to be caught out when the Mandrake he is repotting begins its ear-piercing screams. The earmuffs built into Neville's hair piece block the noise, while an overcoat protects his uniform from dirt.

Mandrake being replanted in a bigger pot

Brick facts

The baby Mandrake root has a unique mold with a stud on top and a pin underneath. Its wrinkly face print is screaming, but the noise it makes won't be fatal until it's older.

Slicked-back blond hair

Draco Malfoy

Harry and Draco got off to a bad start when they first met, and since then their relationship has gone from bad to worse. Now in his sixth year at Hogwarts, Draco is furious that Harry is invited to Professor Slughorn's party and he isn't. Scowling Draco wanders the castle alone in Hogwarts Astronomy Tower (set 75969).

Green-and-silver Slytherin uniform

Hufflepuff tie

Short, nonposable legs

Susan Bones

This cheery minifigure is one of Harry's Hufflepuff classmates, Susan Bones. She's the first minifigure to wear the yellow-and-black Hufflepuff tie. Her smiling face turns around to reveal a worried one: well, she is in Hogwarts Great Hall (set 75954) when the Chamber of Secrets opens!

Freckles on cheeks

Seamus Finnigan

Gryffindor Seamus looks cheerful here, but the other side of his freckled face shows alarm. He appears in Hogwarts Whomping Willow (set 75953), where Harry and Ron come crashing into school in the blue Ford Anglia car.

Dean Thomas

All wrapped up against the cold, Dean Thomas is ready to go and cheer for Gryffindor on the Quidditch pitch. Dean is a big fan of Quidditch, but his real love is soccer, played by Muggles. He brightens up life at Hogwarts with his straight-talking and practical attitude.

Gryffindor lion on flag

Dark-red-and-gold house scarf

Medium-sized posable legs

Quidditch

The roar of the crowd, the flash of broomsticks, the clash of winners and losers, the risk of injury … they all mean one thing: a Hogwarts Quidditch match! Quidditch is the favorite sport of wizards and witches. It's a ball game played on broomsticks and every match is an event that the whole school comes to watch. Harry is a natural at it.

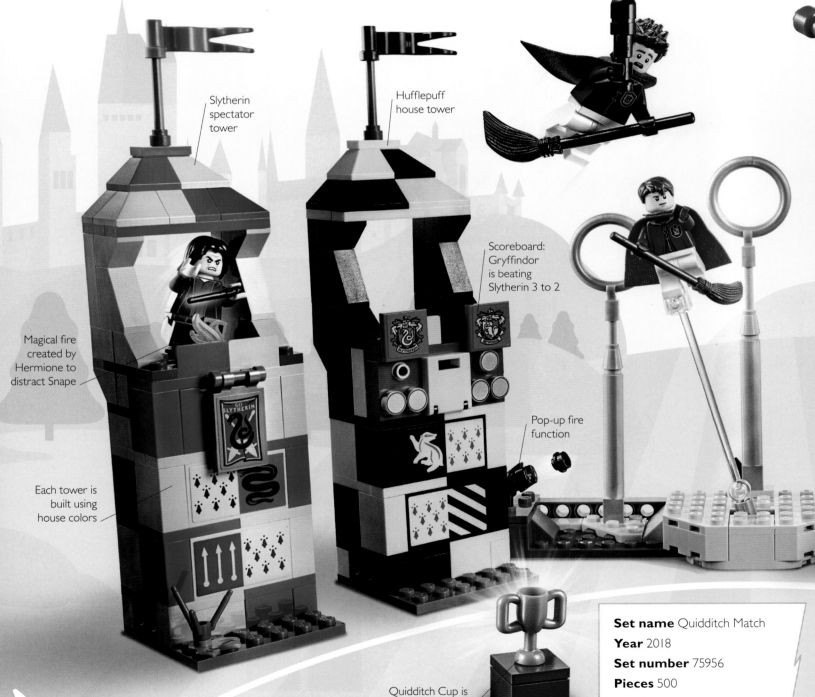

Golden Snitch is worth 150 points when caught

Slytherin spectator tower

Hufflepuff house tower

Scoreboard: Gryffindor is beating Slytherin 3 to 2

Magical fire created by Hermione to distract Snape

Pop-up fire function

Each tower is built using house colors

Quidditch Cup is presented once a year

Set name Quidditch Match
Year 2018
Set number 75956
Pieces 500
Minifigures 6

Game on

Slytherin Chaser Marcus Flint shoots the Quaffle. Can Gryffindor's Keeper, Oliver Wood, keep him from scoring a goal? Meanwhile, Beater Lucian Bole wants to put Harry off his game with a Bludger, or even with his bat. But Harry is already in enough trouble. His broom is behaving very oddly!

On the ball

Quidditch is a game of four balls: the red Quaffle, the Golden Snitch, and two violent black Bludgers. This set, however, comes with extra Bludgers that can be fired at the minifigures from a real stud-shooter.

Red flag tops Gryffindor tower

Ravenclaw supporters' tower

Megaphone for game's commentator

Brick facts

LEGO stud-shooters have been seen on vehicles and even as minifigure-held weapons, but this is the first time one has been mounted on a broomstick.

He shoots ... he scores!

For 10 points, the Quaffle must be thrown through one of three hooped goalposts. Oliver Wood's minifigure is perched on a moving pole to defend all three hoops. Marcus Flint's broom features a shooting function to launch the Quaffle at the goals.

Chest for storing all three types of ball

Hinged door through which players enter the pitch

Quidditch players

All first-year students take flying lessons, but only a few make it onto a house Quidditch team. Seven players from each house are selected to compete for the Quidditch Cup and glory for their team. These players are all speedy on a broom, nimble at dodging missiles, and eagle-eyed.

Wind-ruffled hair piece shared with Seamus Finnigan

Green-and-silver Slytherin robes

Every house wants to win the Quidditch Cup

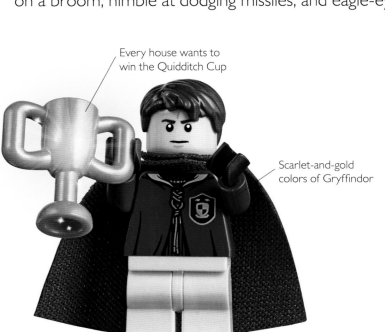

Scarlet-and-gold colors of Gryffindor

Lucian Bole

Armed with a hefty bat in Quidditch Match (set 75956), Lucian Bole is one of Slytherin's two Beaters. His role is to use the bat to hit the Bludgers away from his teammates and toward the other team. But violent Lucian has been known to use his bat directly on rival players.

Oliver Wood

As Gryffindor Captain and Keeper, it's Oliver Wood's job to both lead the team and guard the goal hoops to prevent the other team from scoring goals with the Quaffle. His minifigure has a determined expression and he pushes his players hard to beat the other houses—particularly Slytherin.

Hair piece also on Credence Barebone's minifigure

Toothy snarl directed at the opposition

Torso design is shared by all Slytherin players

Marcus Flint

The Slytherin Quidditch Captain, Marcus Flint is the direct rival of Oliver Wood. Flint drives his team hard as well—but doesn't always make them play by the rules. Until Harry Potter joined the game, Slytherin were the reigning champions—and that's not a title that they'll give up easily.

Spiky gray hair

Madam Hooch

Rolanda Hooch is Hogwarts' flying instructor and Quidditch referee. She's an expert on the subject of broomsticks and her minifigure comes with a brown one. She wears yellow-tinted flying goggles when she shows her students how it's done. The other side of her dual-sided head shows a more stern expression, without goggles.

Brass whistle for refereeing

Black teacher's robes show no house favoritism

Green LEGO broomstick is unique to Draco

Slicked-back blond hair isn't windswept, yet!

Draco Malfoy

Draco Malfoy and Harry Potter don't get along at the best of times, but their rivalry really comes out on the Quidditch pitch. Draco is the Slytherin Seeker, so the two boys are in competition to see who will catch the Golden Snitch first. With his scowling face, Draco looks determined to beat Harry.

Shorter cape than Slytherin teammates

Broom handle fits in a minifigure's hand

Brick facts

Everyone wants to see the tiny Golden Snitch. The glittering prize is worth 150 points, and catching it ends the game. Its exclusive LEGO mold captures its delicate wings and ornate decoration.

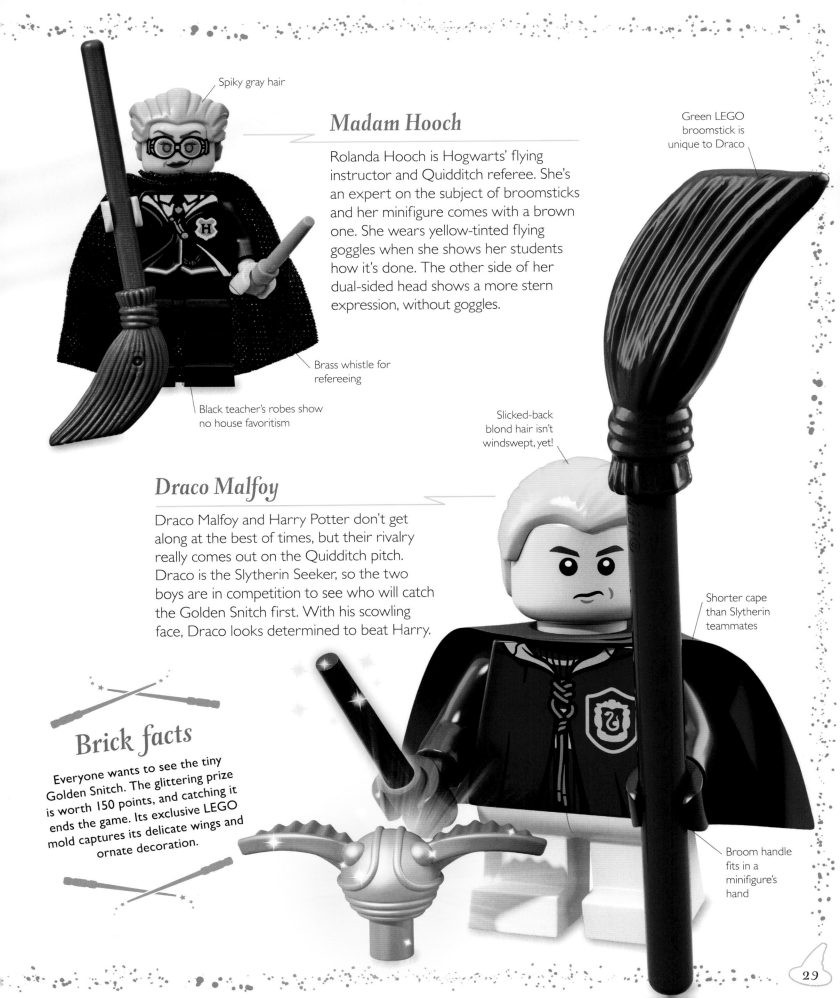

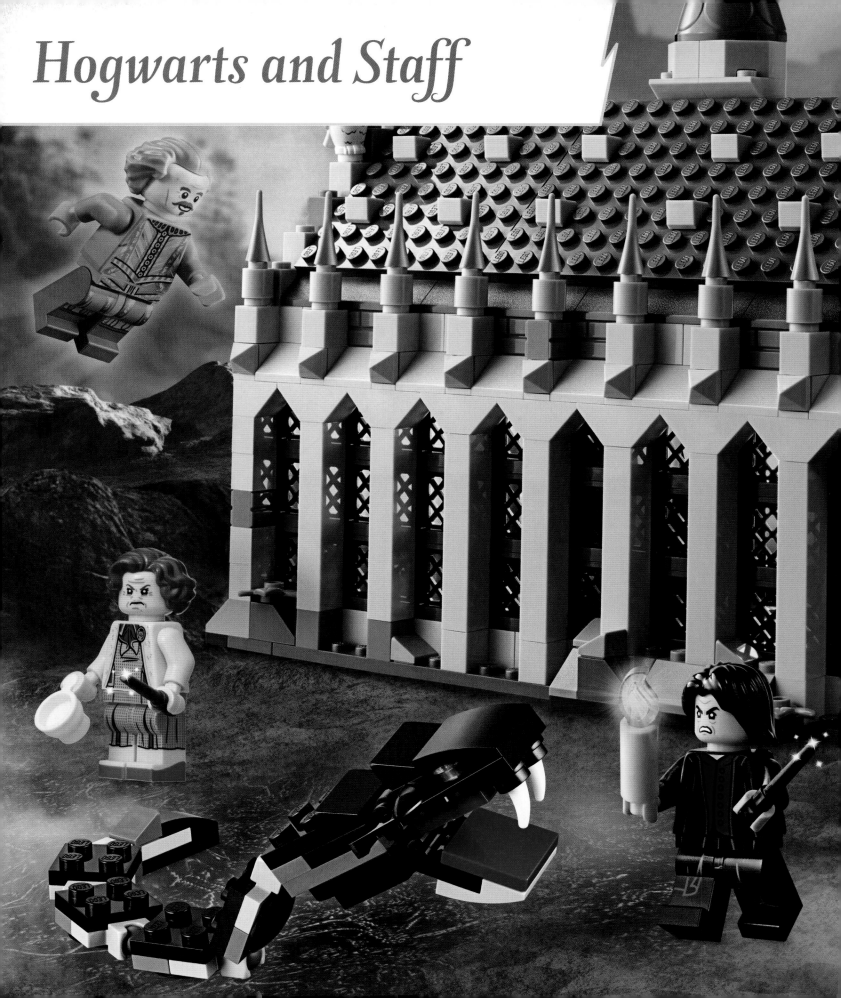

Hogwarts and Staff

Hogwarts castle

Welcome to Hogwarts School of Witchcraft and Wizardry—and congratulations on finding it. This ancient castle of imposing towers and fairy-tale spires perches atop a remote mountain. Its magically disguised location in the Scottish Highlands can't even be plotted on a map. Although more than 1,000 years old, the castle is as strong as ever, sturdily built in stone, and held together by powerful magic.

Microscale castle

This is the most extensive LEGO® set of Hogwarts ever made. Such is the castle's size that even in microscale—smaller proportions than the usual minifigure scale—this model uses more than 6,000 pieces and is 29½ in (75 cm) wide. The set includes minifigures of the four Hogwarts founders, which can be displayed on a separate stand.

Escaped Hungarian Horntail dragon clings to roof tiles

Brick-built cladding covers round panels

Back of a gray tooth piece makes a gable window

Transparent bricks for stained-glass windows

Boathouse

Set name
Hogwarts Castle

Year 2018

Set number
71043

Pieces 6,020

Minifigures 4 (plus 27 microfigures)

The Whomping Willow

This mini-sized Whomping Willow tree in Hogwarts' grounds is tiny, but the branches still move thanks to a few clever LEGO connections. The tree's spiky branches are dark-orange flower stalks, and Arthur Weasley's blue Ford Anglia car is built on top of a minifigure's roller skate piece.

Gray beard

Bald patch

Slytherin house tie

Professor Dumbledore

Argus Filch

Slytherin student

Microfigures

This huge set is inhabited by 27 tiny microscale figures, including staff, students from each house, and even five spooky Dementors! The mold for the figures was first used to make trophies for minifigures to hold. Its base fits onto a single stud.

Turrets of different sizes top stone towers

Microfigures walk over viaduct

Evergreen trees are upside-down flower stems stacked on a pole

Hagrid's hut

The hut where the half-giant Hagrid lives often seems too small for him, but this version is particularly petite. Hagrid's two rooms sit on octagonal rings, and single studs make enormous pumpkins in the garden. At this scale, a regular spider piece can represent the huge Acromantula known as Aragog, who dwells in the Forbidden Forest.

Hogwarts founders

More than 1,000 years ago, four witches and wizards came together with a shared idea: they wanted to create the best magic school in the world. This is how Hogwarts School of Witchcraft and Wizardry came to be. Each founder gave their name to a house that celebrates key aspects of their personality, which students are still sorted into centuries later.

Diadem was later lost for centuries

Starry-night pattern

Rowena Ravenclaw

Brainy students follow in the footsteps of Rowena Ravenclaw. An exceptionally clever witch, she favored students with the sharpest minds. The values of learning and wisdom live on in Ravenclaws today, who follow the motto engraved onto their founder's diadem: "Wit beyond measure is man's greatest treasure."

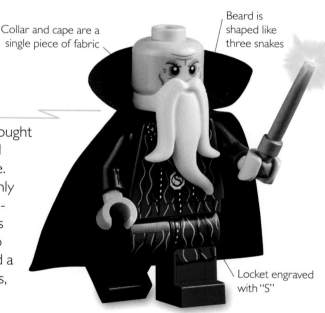

Collar and cape are a single piece of fabric

Beard is shaped like three snakes

Locket engraved with "S"

Salazar Slytherin

Cunning Salazar Slytherin sought out the most ambitious and talented pupils for his house. But most importantly, he only wanted students from pure-blood wizarding families. His desire to close Hogwarts to anyone Muggle-born caused a split with the other founders, and eventually he left.

Basilisk

Before Salazar Slytherin left Hogwarts, he built a room deep in the castle. The room was called the Chamber of Secrets and it held the monstrous Basilisk. It is deadly to look this huge serpent in its eyes. Its sharp fangs have useful magical properties.

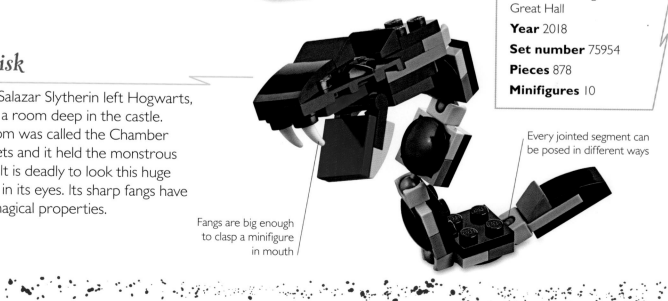

Every jointed segment can be posed in different ways

Fangs are big enough to clasp a minifigure in mouth

Set name Hogwarts Great Hall
Year 2018
Set number 75954
Pieces 878
Minifigures 10

Godric Gryffindor

As bold and brave as a lion, Godric also looked a little like his house's symbol with his bushy, mane-like hair and beard. He faced every situation with great courage and founded his house for "those with brave deeds to their name." It's no surprise that Harry, Ron, and Hermione are all Gryffindors!

Hufflepuff cup later became a Horcrux

Badger symbol on clasp for cape

Robes are elegant but not showy

Red version of Nearly Headless Nick and Ollivander's hair

Sword of Gryffindor was made by goblins

Helga Hufflepuff

While her fellow teachers concerned themselves with teaching the cleverest or the most courageous, Helga Hufflepuff just wanted her students to be fair and loyal and to apply themselves. And in return, she offered them equally fair treatment, saying "I'll teach the lot and treat them just the same."

House banners

In Hogwarts Great Hall (set 75954), two double-sided banners hang down over long tables. Each house is celebrated with its own symbol and colors: blue-and-gray Ravenclaw has an eagle, green-and-silver Slytherin has a snake, gold-and-scarlet Gryffindor has a lion, and yellow-and-black Hufflepuff has a badger.

Ravenclaw

Slytherin

Gryffindor

Hufflepuff

The Great Hall

The imposing size of Hogwarts castle and its peculiar magical ways can be a little overwhelming on first encounter. New students are taken immediately to the Great Hall to be sorted into one of the four Hogwarts houses. For Harry, who never felt like he belonged with the Dursleys, Hogwarts is the best place he's ever known and soon feels like home—despite the curious floating candles and moving staircases!

Mirror of Erised has swappable panels

The Sorting Hat

Hermione carries Potions cauldron

Brick facts

This 1x1 brick with a scroll has added grandeur to LEGO sets since 2015. Perfect for Hogwarts' ornate architecture, it features in pale yellow for stone and in brown for wood.

Home away from home

The Great Hall set includes a dining room with four long tables for students and the raised High Table for teachers. At one end of the Hall is a four-story tower with a Potions classroom, a room with treasure, and an attic in the turret. The set draws inspiration from Harry's adventures in his first two years at Hogwarts.

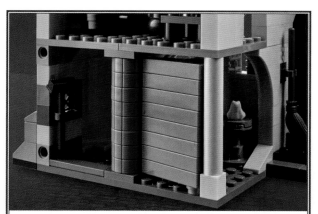

Spiraling staircase

Hogwarts' staircases are known for moving while people are still on them. Here, minifigures can pass between the ground floor and the Potions room—if the stairs will allow it! The steps are threaded onto a column and can be stacked or fanned into a spiral. When the steps are tucked in, Filch's broom cupboard is revealed.

The Sorting Hat

Upon arriving at Hogwarts, every student is put into one of the school's four houses in the Sorting Ceremony. The magical Sorting Hat is placed on each young witch or wizard's head. The hat may be ancient and scruffy, but it's incredibly wise and can determine which house each student is best suited to.

Folds in the hat create a face

Set name Hogwarts Great Hall
Year 2018
Set number 75954
Pieces 878
Minifigures 10

School life

The Great Hall, with its large fireplace, is where students gather three times a day to eat meals. It's also where announcements are made and special celebrations are held. It is a good thing there is plenty of room, as the set comes with ten minifigures, including Professor Quirrell and Susan Bones.

Owls deliver mail to the Great Hall

"Floating" candles

House banners are double-sided

Harry battles Draco in a Dueling Club encounter

40 square window grilles are included in the set

Professor McGonagall sits at the teachers' table

Susan Bones enjoys a cup of tea

Albus Dumbledore

Nobody embodies Hogwarts School of Witchcraft and Wizardry as much as its headmaster, Albus Percival Wulfric Brian Dumbledore. He is a wizard of great power and wisdom. His kindly smile and twinkling eyes reassure his students.

The legendary Elder Wand cannot be defeated

Gold half-moon glasses

Hogwarts headmaster

In LEGO Hogwarts Great Hall (set 75954), Dumbledore's distinguished minifigure wears rich maroon robes with printed metallic whirls that give them a touch of magic. Dumbledore is the only LEGO minifigure with this light-gray beard piece.

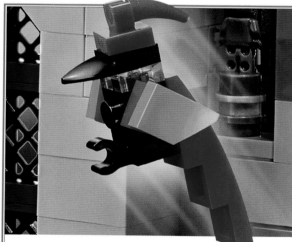

Fawkes the Phoenix

Fawkes is a scarlet Phoenix who lives in Dumbledore's office. When Phoenixes die, they burst into flames and are reborn from their own ashes. This LEGO Fawkes can also break up and be rebuilt for another adventure. The red plume on his head is a LEGO claw piece.

Beard printing on face

Brick facts

Dumbledore's minifigures have two types of beard. The later one, which has a band tied around the lower part of his beard, was new in 2018 and is exclusive to his character.

Dancing Dumbledore

On Christmas Eve of Harry's fourth year, Dumbledore dresses in his fanciest lavender robes for the Yule Ball. He enjoys the celebration with a friendly, relaxed face. If anything should go wrong, his head can be turned around to look concerned—or maybe tired after dancing the night away.

Embroidered gold edging

Headmaster's study

In Hogwarts Clock Tower (set 75948), Dumbledore ponders the important magical questions of the day at his ornate desk. On the wall behind him are stickers of the Sorting Hat and Fawkes the Phoenix. The stone Pensieve stands on his right, and the Sword of Gryffindor is mounted on the wall above his head.

Hat with a gold tassel is molded to a new hair piece

Bowl piece has a unique Pensieve print with swirling memory pattern

Thoughtful wizard

Peer into the swirling contents of a Pensieve and you'll be sucked into the memory stored within it. Dumbledore keeps a large, stone Pensieve in his office and his minifigure holds it safely. The blue swirls match his embroidered blue robes.

Instead of legs, Dumbledore has an elegantly curved LEGO slope piece for his long robe

Within Hogwarts

Hogwarts is held together with powerful spells and charms—some of which even Dumbledore hasn't uncovered. Bathilda Bagshot's book *Hogwarts: A History* reveals some secrets—for example, that the Great Hall's ceiling is enchanted to look like the night sky. Other secrets Harry and his friends must uncover for themselves as they explore the ancient castle.

Brick facts

This piece was originally used by minifigures as a ski pole, but here it's a mint green color and upside down. It tops each of Hogwarts' spires, fitting into a small cone to connect it to the larger turrets.

Architecture in miniature

Although this LEGO set is built to microscale, it captures the grandeur of Hogwarts castle, with high ceilings, Roman and Gothic arches, colorful stained glass, ornate stonework, and soaring spires. The rooms, scenes, and characters within are inspired by Harry's first five years at Hogwarts.

Writing on the wall says "The Chamber of Secrets has been opened. Enemies of the heir beware."

School library

Brush up on Transfiguration or get extra help with tricky Potions homework in the library. One-plate-thick brown bookshelves alternate with colored books, and there are desks with seats for studious microfigures—including a bookworm Hermione, of course!

Bellatrix Lestrange lurks in the Room of Requirement

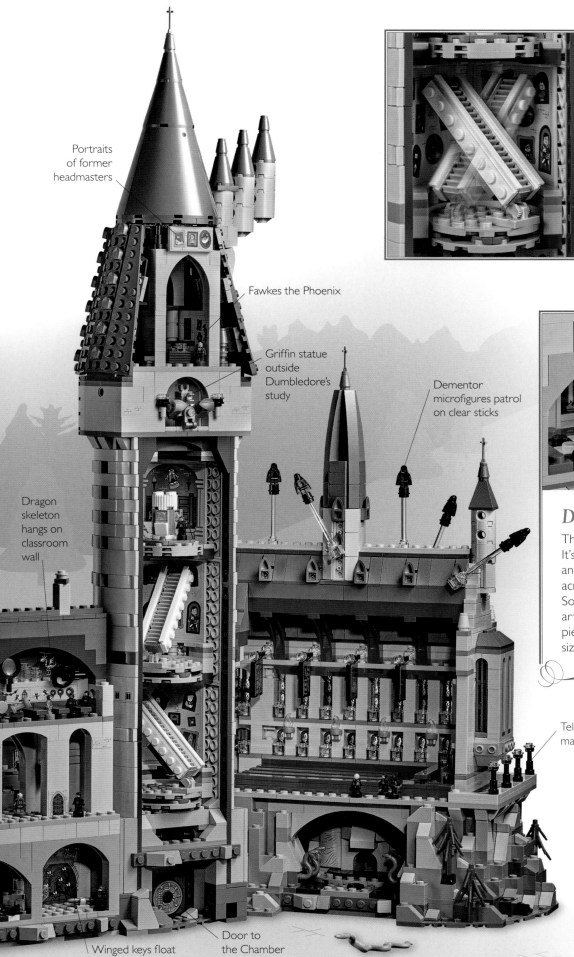

Portraits of former headmasters

Fawkes the Phoenix

Griffin statue outside Dumbledore's study

Dragon skeleton hangs on classroom wall

Dementor microfigures patrol on clear sticks

Winged keys float on transparent tiles

Door to the Chamber of Secrets

Telescope piece makes a lamppost

Spinning staircases

Finding your way around the vast castle is hard enough without the stairs conspiring against you, too. Hogwarts is famous for its 142 enchanted staircases that move at will. Thanks to turntable and hinged connections, these stairs can completely change direction.

Deadly chessboard

This is no ordinary wizards' chessboard. It's a game of life and death! Harry, Ron, and Hermione must play their way across it as real pieces to reach the Sorcerer's Stone, a precious wizarding artifact. Two of the enchanted playing pieces are plain microfigures—the same size as Harry, Ron, and Hermione.

Set name Hogwarts Castle

Year 2018

Set number 71043

Pieces 6,020

Minifigures 4 (plus 27 microfigures)

Heads of house

The house system at Hogwarts divides students up into four groups. Each house has its own common room and student bedrooms. A professor leads each house as its head, caring for those pupils who belong to it. This means being kind but also strict, and sometimes punishing students who misbehave.

Brick facts

The heads of Slytherin, Gryffindor, and Ravenclaw houses appeared as LEGO minifigures in 2018. Perhaps Professor Sprout, head of Hufflepuff house, was busy repotting plants in her greenhouse!

Professor Snape

Head of Slytherin House, Severus Snape embodies two of the worst things about Harry's time at school: Slytherin enemies and Snape himself. The Potions master is an imposing figure, even in LEGO form, and he appears to revel in making Harry's life miserable. However, he has been known to help Harry out in a crisis.

Fierce expression is slightly less mad on the other side

Wand is used to help Harry in Quidditch Match (set 75956)

Snape the Boggart

Boggart creatures take the form you find most frightening, and for Neville Longbottom that means Professor Snape. However, a spell to dress the Snape-Boggart in Neville's grandmother's robes, hat, and fox stole makes it look ridiculous—and far less scary. Boggart defeated!

Professor McGonagall

Transfiguration teacher Minerva McGonagall is the head of Gryffindor house. Firm but fair, she doesn't allow any nonsense from anyone. Students occasionally feel her wrath and she isn't afraid to stand up to officials who interfere with the running of the school, either. She's stern but can show great warmth to the pupils under her care.

Traditional witch's hat

Jeweled brooch

Emerald-green robes

Bow tie piece can be removed

Megaphone is used by Flitwick at the Yule Ball

Fabric coat tails touch the ground

Professor Flitwick

Filius Flitwick is as intelligent as you'd expect the head of brainy Ravenclaw house to be. He's an expert Charms master as well as a dueling champion. Part-goblin, his minifigures have short, nonposable legs, and he's always very neatly dressed in a three-piece suit, dress shirt, and bow tie.

Choir master

In the LEGO® Harry Potter™ Advent Calendar (set 75964), Professor Flitwick has taken off his jacket so he can conduct the Hogwarts festive choir more easily. His open mouth sings along merrily with his students.

Hogwarts staff

Teachers are an important part of the Hogwarts school community, living and working in the school for many years. The wizarding world can be a little overwhelming to young wizards and witches. There is so much to learn, and you don't want to mix up Spleenwart with Sneezewort or fail to recognize exploding Erumpent Fluid. Hogwarts staff are here to help—though some more so than others.

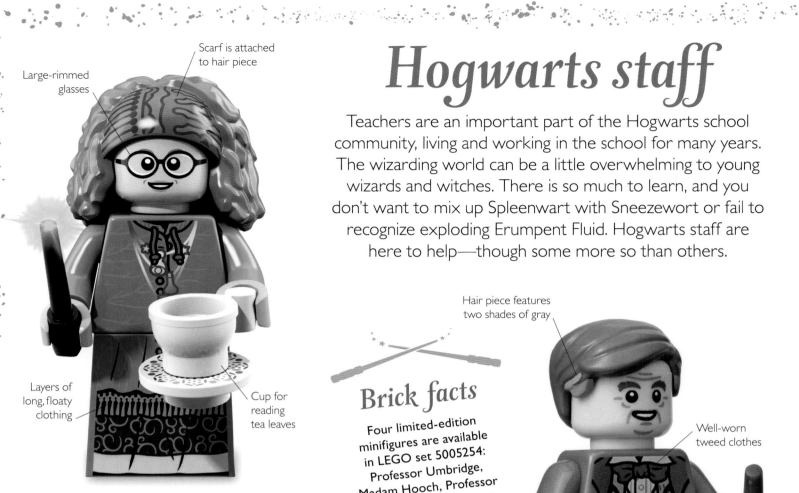

Large-rimmed glasses

Scarf is attached to hair piece

Layers of long, floaty clothing

Cup for reading tea leaves

Professor Trelawney

Sybill Trelawney is a Seer, which means she can predict the future. Her skill is much weaker than her great-great grandmother's was, however Sybill has learned tricks over the years to cover her shortcomings. She teaches Divination, which includes reading the stars, tea leaves, and dreams.

Brick facts

Four limited-edition minifigures are available in LEGO set 5005254: Professor Umbridge, Madam Hooch, Professor Slughorn, and a Boggart imitating Professor Snape.

Hair piece features two shades of gray

Well-worn tweed clothes

Felix Felicis potion is also called Liquid Luck

Potions master

Professor Slughorn takes on the job of Potions master in Harry's sixth year at Hogwarts. Slughorn mixes work and leisure in Hogwarts Astronomy Tower (set 75969). He studies a Potions textbook in the classroom, but also throws a party, complete with a chocolate fountain!

Professor Slughorn

Students who are gifted at Potions will do well in Horace Slughorn's class. But they'll do even better if Slughorn thinks that they're a valuable addition to his collection of Very Important People. Those who make the grade receive an invitation to his exclusive "Slug Club."

Nearly Headless Nick

Poor Sir Nicholas de Mimsy-Porpington. Since his execution 500 years ago, he's been called Nearly Headless Nick because his head wasn't completely cut off. The minifigure version of the Ghost of Gryffindor Tower can have his head removed and placed on his hand with the ease of any other LEGO connection.

Head clips snugly onto hand

Ghostly body printed in silver and black over gray

Fifteenth-century style jacket

Hair piece is worn in blonde by Queenie Goldstein

Brooch with a kitten

Pink high heels

Professor Umbridge

Do not be fooled by this friendly-looking woman. Underneath the pink, fluffy, frilly clothes and love of kittens, Dolores Umbridge is a cruel, mean witch. She comes to Hogwarts to teach Defense Against the Dark Arts, but she secretly has her own plans for Hogwarts and its students.

Bald patch and hair attach on top of head as one piece

Scruffy waistcoat

Filch

Argus Filch is happiest when he's prowling the corridors with his cat, Mrs. Norris, or gleefully getting students into trouble. Under bushy eyebrows, his eyes are on constant lookout for rule-breaking students. He wears a long, gray overcoat to protect his clothes from dust and dirt.

Keys to Hogwarts' doors

Rubeus Hagrid

Towering over other minifigures, this half-giant and half-wizard is Rubeus Hagrid—Keeper of Keys and Grounds at Hogwarts. He may seem rather gruff, but really he is a sensitive soul who sees the gentle side of all creatures (even those others would find alarming!). Hagrid takes Harry under his wing and is fiercely loyal to both him and Dumbledore.

Secret spell-maker?

Hagrid hasn't been allowed to do magic with a wand since he was expelled from Hogwarts and his wand was broken. However, it's rumored that he carries the wand pieces around with him, hidden inside his pink umbrella.

Bushy, tangled hair

Oversize moleskin coat

Deep, molded pockets to carry gamekeeper tools

Arms have the same movement as regular minifigure arms

Brick facts

Hagrid's shaggy mass of brown hair swamps his regular-size minifigure head. His eyes peek out through the single hair-moustache-and-beard piece, which isn't seen on any other character.

Gentle giant

Hagrid's LEGO figure clips together differently from standard minifigures. He has short nonposable legs, but he stands taller thanks to his large, custom-made, solid body piece. He appears in Hagrid's Hut: Buckbeak's Rescue (set 75947) and Hogwarts Great Hall (set 75954).

LEGO arrow piece tops each roof peak

Each section of the roof is made with two angle plates

Hagrid's Hut

After work, Hagrid doesn't need to leave his beloved Hogwarts because he lives in the castle grounds in his own cozy hut. The LEGO set is opened up into two half-rooms with easy access for playing. Inside, Hagrid's tools hang from the rafters and the fireplace glows with a brick that really lights up.

Both doors open and are tall enough for Hagrid to pass through

Set name Hagrid's Hut: Buckbeak's Rescue

Year 2019

Set number 75947

Pieces 496

Minifigures 6

Olive-green vines grow in the stonework

Time for tea

Harry, Ron, and Hermione are always welcome in Hagrid's hut. It's a cozy place to chat, so long as they don't mind spiders in the rafters and a dragon egg in the fireplace. Hagrid can be a useful source of information—even if he doesn't always mean to be.

Refreshing cup of tea

Furry dress robes with extra-furry trim

Dressed to impress

Even Hagrid makes an effort to dress up sometimes. He swaps his moleskin overcoat for furry dress robes, a shirt, and a polka-dot tie to greet Madame Maxime in Beauxbatons' Carriage: Arrival at Hogwarts (set 75958). He still looks rather scruffy, but he is very warm and welcoming.

Hogwarts grounds

Hogwarts was built in a remote, far-flung location, away from prying Muggle eyes. Apart from the small village of Hogsmeade, there is no one else for miles around, but it's not a boring place. The surrounding countryside is perfect for studying magical plants and creatures in their natural habitats. However, minifigures must be careful: the grounds of Hogwarts are not always safe.

Set name Forbidden Forest: Umbridge's Takedown
Year 2020
Set number 75967
Pieces 253
Minifigures 3

Baby Acromantula

Tree opens to store accessories

Poisonous fungus

LEGO tooth pieces for shaggy hair

1×2 jumper plate is belly button

Giant hand carries a shrieking Professor Umbridge

Grawp the giant

Stay away from the Forbidden Forest. It bristles with magic and many dangers lurk among its dark trees, not least Hagrid's "baby" half-brother, Grawp. Hagrid is trying to teach the brutish young giant some manners in the hope of making him less aggressive, but it doesn't seem to be working.

Brown shoot piece at the end of each branch

Articulated arms flail around violently

Brick facts

This curved, organic shape has been used for plant stems and roots as well as in different colors for a dog tail, a pig tail, a frog tongue, dragon details, and sea creature tentacles.

Set name Hogwarts Whomping Willow

Year 2018

Set number 75953

Pieces 753

Minifigures 6

Gear mechanism causes all the branches to spin

The Whomping Willow

In contrast to the branches of weeping willow trees, which bend over to the ground, the magical Whomping Willow lashes out at anything within whacking distance. Planted to protect a secret entrance to the Shrieking Shack, the tree attacks anyone who comes near with its vicious, whirling branches.

The Great Lake

"This way to the boats!" calls Hagrid as he accompanies new first-year pupils from Hogsmeade Station to school. These students are crossing the deep, icy waters of the Great Lake in a pre-molded boat with a tall lantern holder. The boat has no oars— it rows itself magically.

Set name Hogwarts Great Hall

Year 2018

Set number 75954

Pieces 878

Minifigures 10

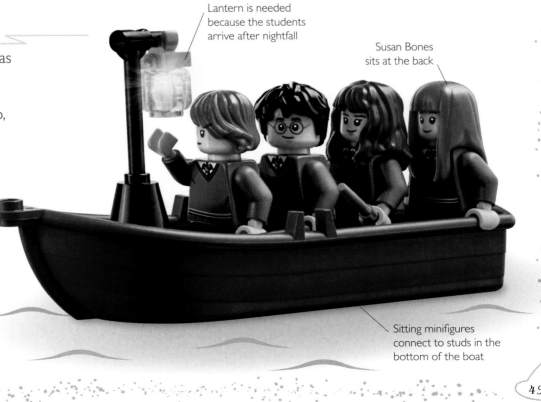

Lantern is needed because the students arrive after nightfall

Susan Bones sits at the back

Sitting minifigures connect to studs in the bottom of the boat

Wizarding World

Diagon Alley

Witches and wizards who want to do a spot of window shopping or stock up on broom-cupboard essentials head to Diagon Alley. In this set, a selection of small, colorful pieces captures the variety of the street's architecture. The shops are built in microscale, and the street-scene set comes with a minifigure of Diagon Alley's most famous shopkeeper: Mr. Ollivander.

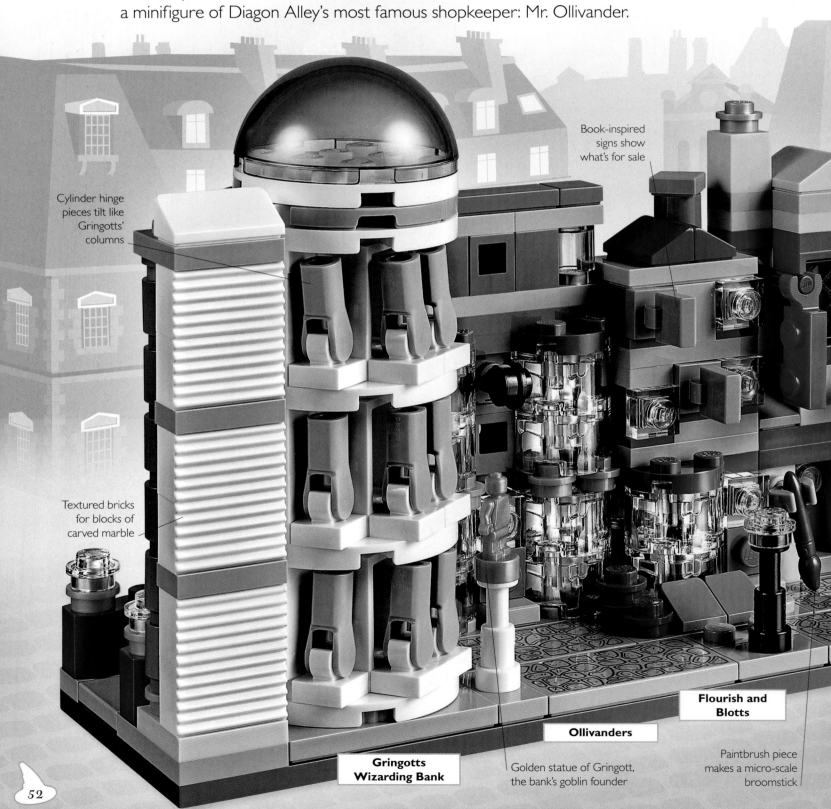

Book-inspired signs show what's for sale

Cylinder hinge pieces tilt like Gringotts' columns

Textured bricks for blocks of carved marble

Flourish and Blotts

Ollivanders

Gringotts Wizarding Bank

Golden statue of Gringott, the bank's goblin founder

Paintbrush piece makes a micro-scale broomstick

Shopping street

At one end of the street lies the marble-columned facade of Gringotts Wizarding Bank. Alongside the bank sit the world-renowned Ollivanders wand shop, Flourish and Blotts bookstore, and Quality Quidditch Supplies. To the right of an arched alleyway is a joke shop named Weasleys' Wizard Wheezes—owned by Ron's twin brothers, Fred and George.

Surprise find

Fred and George's joke shop looks fun and lively, even from the street. A grinning face greets customers by raising his hat. In this set, the top hat is attached to an unusual LEGO® black sausage piece that creates just the right angle—and a surprise worthy of the Weasley brothers themselves!

Lavender top hat piece is very rare

Brick facts

Headlight bricks are used for Diagon Alley's tiny microscale windows. They can make both round and square windows depending on placement. This set contains gray, green, and orange examples.

Curved bay windows

Receding hair piece shared with Nearly Headless Nick

Overgrown gray sideburns

Weasleys' Wizard Wheezes

Exclusive plate with a cobblestone print

Quality Quidditch Supplies

Entrance to Knockturn Alley

Set name Diagon Alley
Year 2018
Set number 40289
Pieces 374
Minifigures 1

Garrick Ollivander

The Ollivander family has been selling wands on Diagon Alley for centuries. The current Mr. Ollivander has sold wands to almost every Hogwarts student and their parents—though of course, it is the wand that chooses the wizard. His minifigure shows his age and his antique taste in clothes.

Magical community

Harry and his friends are away at school for much of the year, but they aren't completely cut off from the outside world. As he grows older, Harry meets many members of the wider wizarding world. Some are welcome new friends, such Harry's godfather, Sirius Black, and the house-elf, Dobby. Others, including the spooky Dementors, Harry would rather avoid!

Bald head with batlike ears is made from rubbery plastic

Sock is Dobby's key to freedom

Tom Riddle's diary has damage from a Basilisk fang

Dobby

House-elves usually serve a wizard family, but Dobby is a free elf thanks to Harry Potter. Harry tricked Lucius Malfoy into releasing Dobby by giving him a sock hidden in a book. Until this point, Dobby had only worn a pillowcase, as depicted on his threadbare minifigure printing.

Werewolf scratches on face

Remus Lupin

Professor Lupin teaches Defense Against the Dark Arts in Harry's third year, but he is hiding a secret. Once a month he turns into a ferocious werewolf. This is hinted at by his alternative face printing that shows Lupin beginning the transformation into a werewolf. Lupin was friends with Harry's parents at school and helps Harry perfect spells to repel Dementors.

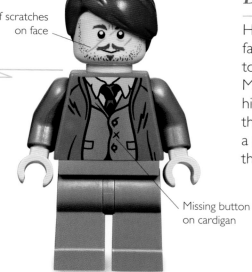

Missing button on cardigan

Replacement eye can see through objects and spin 360 degrees

Mad-Eye Moody

Alastor "Mad-Eye" Moody works to protect the wizarding world from Dark forces, but even this expert has fallen victim to them. The Dark wizard Barty Crouch, Jr., has been known to impersonate Moody to gain access to Hogwarts and cause trouble for Harry.

Metallic silver prosthetic leg

Brick facts

Moody carries a flask of Polyjuice Potion, made from a recolored LEGO maraca piece. He transforms into Barty Crouch, Jr., with a twist of his head and a new hair piece.

Scruffy beard after long stay in prison

Striped prison clothes

Sirius Black

Harry's godfather is Sirius Black. His minifigure has to keep a low profile because he escaped from Azkaban prison after being locked up for a crime he didn't commit. Sirius Black is an Animagus and can magically transform to take the form of a large, shaggy dog.

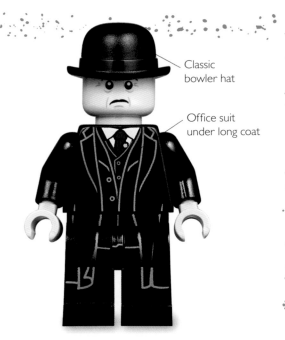

Classic bowler hat

Office suit under long coat

Nymphadora Tonks

Tonks could have no end of minifigures: as a Metamorphmagus she can change her appearance at will. A vibrant, young Auror (a hunter of Dark wizards), she's a brave member of the Order of the Phoenix and helps protect Harry in Attack on the Burrow (set 75980). She marries Lupin, unfazed by his werewolf condition.

Decorative silk scarf

Metal studs on clothing

Cornelius Fudge

As Minister of Magic, Cornelius Fudge should enjoy lots of power, but Dark influences are disrupting his rule. His minifigure is right to look worried—he can only pretend everything is okay for so long before he loses control of his government.

Dementor

Ghastly Dementors feed on happiness. These floating fiends are supposed to guard the prison Azkaban. However, some leave to go in search of the escaped prisoner, Sirius Black. One Dementor boards the Hogwarts Express (set 75955) and attacks Harry Potter. Fortunately, Dementors can be repelled by the Patronus charm.

Eyeless face—Dementors navigate by sensing people's feelings

Mouth ready to steal a soul with a Dementor's Kiss

Ragged cape

Twisted, smoke-like base

The Knight Bus

Welcome to the Knight Bus—emergency transportation for the stranded witch or wizard. Stick out your wand at the curbside and in moments, this towering purple bus will appear and take you wherever you want to go. It provides a fast service, but not a smooth one. Minifigures had better hold on to their hats and hair pieces—they're in for a bumpy ride!

Magic bus

Built in the style of an old-fashioned London bus, but with an extra third deck, the Knight Bus has been on the road since 1865. The bus adapts to the space available, squeezing itself through narrow gaps and bending around tight corners. Equally adaptable, one side of the LEGO model hinges open for easy access.

Brick facts

The driver travels with a very talkative shrunken head. It's a minifigure head piece with a shriveled face on one side and dreadlocks on the other. It swings around as the bus moves.

KNiGHT BUS

OLD 71

Set name The Knight Bus

Year 2019

Set number 75957

Pieces 403

Minifigures 3

Large headlights for nighttime driving

Even the hubcaps are purple!

Roof comes off easily

3x3 window frame is a brand-new LEGO piece

Bon voyage!

The bus has seats for daytime travel and beds for nighttime journeys. This LEGO bus features a bed on rails so it slides up and down as the bus lurches. Luckily, minifigures don't risk falling out of bed thanks to the brick-built covers. An elaborate chandelier swings from its fitting as the bus bumps along.

Ticket machine slung around shoulder

Stan Shunpike

With a uniform as purple as the bus he works on, Stan Shunpike is the conductor. In Harry's third year at Hogwarts, Stan sells Harry a ticket from his home in Privet Drive to the Leaky Cauldron pub. A ticket to any destination costs 11 sickles, or 13 sickles including hot chocolate—but don't spill it!

Stan clutches *The Daily Prophet* newspaper

ALL DESTINATIONS
(NOTHING UNDERWATER)

Stan holds onto the pole at the rear entrance of the bus

Bald patch and white hair are a single piece

Ernie Prang

Elderly, white-haired wizard Ernie is the driver of the Knight Bus. He wears large, thick glasses to help him see the road. Ernie also gets a running commentary of what lies ahead from the shrunken head that dangles next to his seat.

Base is built very low to the ground

Magical creatures

It's not just wizards and witches who are kept hidden from Muggle eyes. There is a whole world of strange and wonderful creatures that would shock Muggles to discover. Muggles might recognize the Acromantula from the spiders in their bathrooms (although on a much bigger scale!), but dragons, centaurs, and Hippogriffs are usually thought to be the stuff of legend.

Set name Forbidden Forest: Umbridge's Takedown

Year 2020

Set number 75967

Pieces 253

Minifigures 3

Quiver of arrows

Regular minifigure torso piece

Centaur

Centaurs are an ancient species with a proud character. They certainly don't like to be referred to as half-human and half-horse. They're skilled at Divination, Astronomy, and healing. Centaurs shun humans, but Harry and Hermione meet some on a trip into the Forbidden Forest.

Post and chain stop Buckbeak flying away

Buckbeak

Poor Buckbeak is a proud Hippogriff who upset Draco Malfoy and has now been sentenced to death. Half-horse and half-eagle, Hippogriffs are very quick to attack if they feel they have been insulted. Buckbeak is now tied up in Hagrid's pumpkin patch, but Hermione has a plan to save him.

Minifigure can attach for riding

Minifigure head piece in orange

Set name Hagrid's Hut: Buckbeak's Rescue

Year 2019

Set number 75947

Pieces 496

Minifigures 6

Green flower piece is used as pumpkin stem

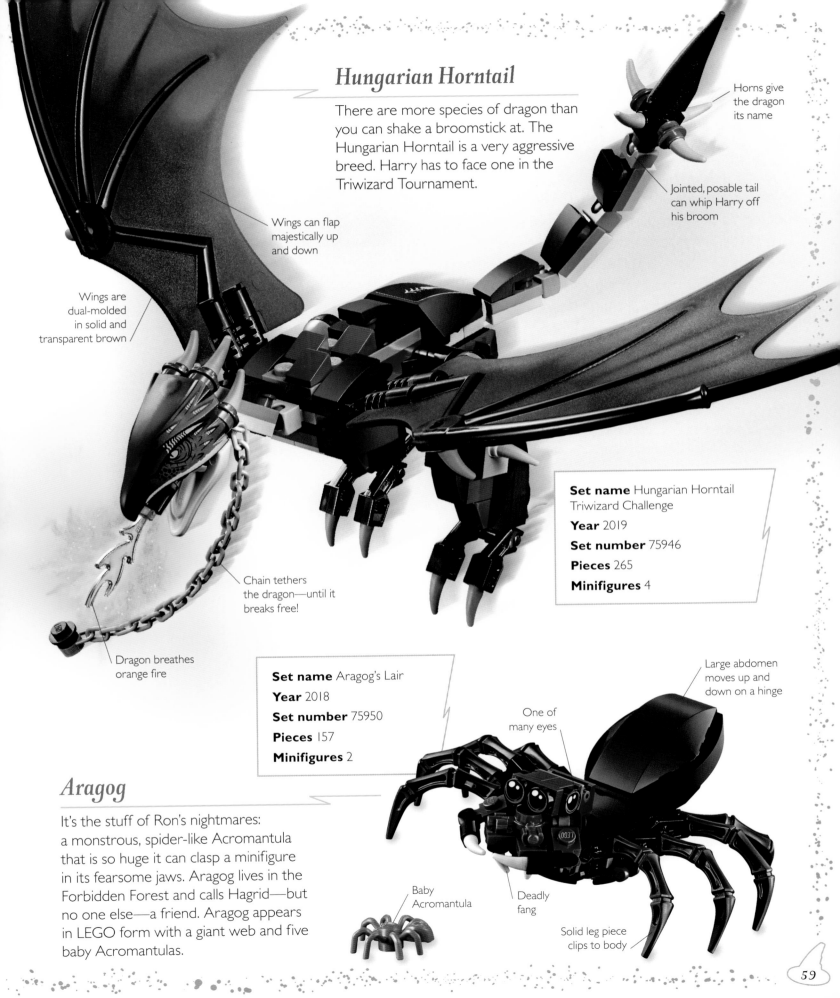

Hungarian Horntail

There are more species of dragon than you can shake a broomstick at. The Hungarian Horntail is a very aggressive breed. Harry has to face one in the Triwizard Tournament.

Horns give the dragon its name

Jointed, posable tail can whip Harry off his broom

Wings can flap majestically up and down

Wings are dual-molded in solid and transparent brown

Set name Hungarian Horntail Triwizard Challenge
Year 2019
Set number 75946
Pieces 265
Minifigures 4

Chain tethers the dragon—until it breaks free!

Dragon breathes orange fire

Set name Aragog's Lair
Year 2018
Set number 75950
Pieces 157
Minifigures 2

Large abdomen moves up and down on a hinge

One of many eyes

Aragog

It's the stuff of Ron's nightmares: a monstrous, spider-like Acromantula that is so huge it can clasp a minifigure in its fearsome jaws. Aragog lives in the Forbidden Forest and calls Hagrid—but no one else—a friend. Aragog appears in LEGO form with a giant web and five baby Acromantulas.

Baby Acromantula

Deadly fang

Solid leg piece clips to body

Triwizard Tournament

The ancient Triwizard Tournament is a grueling test for young wizards and witches. Three students are selected to be champions, one from each of three European schools: Hogwarts, Beauxbatons Academy of Magic, and the Durmstrang Institute. They compete in three difficult and dangerous tasks to see who will be the ultimate Triwizard champion.

Tournament tent

This small but elegant LEGO tent is put up in Hogwarts' grounds for the first Triwizard task. It opens and closes on hinges to provide a refuge where the champions can try to relax, away from the watching eyes of the excited spectators.

The first challenge

For the first task, each champion must retrieve a golden egg that is being guarded by a huge, ferocious dragon. Perhaps the hardest part is the waiting beforehand. At least the champions have their own tent where they can rest and prepare. Inside the shared tent is a bed, refreshments, and drawers for storing belongings.

One wall is decorated with the Durmstrang and Beauxbatons school crests

Set name Hungarian Horntail Triwizard Challenge

Year 2019

Set number 75946

Pieces 265

Minifigures 4

Viktor Krum waits for his turn to face a dragon

Harry Potter

Harry didn't choose to compete in the tournament, but he's forced to take part by mysterious Dark forces. He wears black robes with sleeves in Gryffindor red. Harry puts his Quidditch skills to good use, swooping in to snatch the egg while dodging the dragon on his Firebolt broomstick.

Golden egg

In the heart of each dragon's lair is a nest with a fiercely protected egg. Each contestant must outwit or outrun the dragon to get the prize, which holds their clue to the second task. The LEGO egg shines with a metallic gold finish and is not seen in any other set.

Hogwarts school crest

Much-needed refreshments

"TRI-WIZ-ARD" engraved on cup

Triwizard Cup

Everyone wants to get their hands on the Triwizard Cup, but it is competitor Cedric Diggory who grasps this LEGO version in the LEGO® Harry Potter™ Minifigure Series. Poor Cedric doesn't know that the cup has been enchanted by a Dark wizard!

Triwizard contestants

Traditionally, three champions compete against each other in the Triwizard Tournament. The champions are their schools' best examples of courage, strength, and magical skill. However, this year Harry Potter was mysteriously selected by the Goblet of Fire as a fourth champion, along with a student from each of the three schools.

Hufflepuff hero

Cedric tackles the first tournament task in long yellow-and-black Hufflepuff robes. He wears thick gray gloves to grab the golden egg guarded by a savage Swedish Short-Snout dragon. He uses Transfiguration to distract the dragon and just gets away in time.

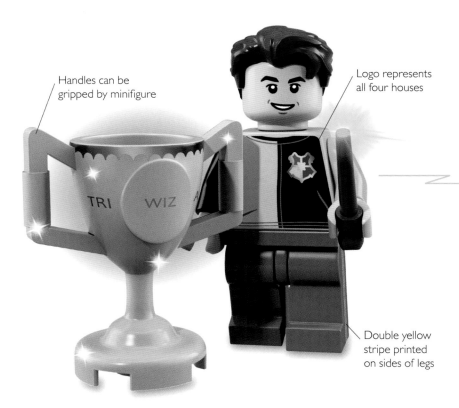

Handles can be gripped by minifigure

Logo represents all four houses

Double yellow stripe printed on sides of legs

Cedric Diggory

The original Hogwarts champion, Cedric is a very popular student. He's in the sixth year and has succeeded both in the classroom and out of it. He has been a prefect, Quidditch Seeker, and captain of the Hufflepuff team. Dressed in Hufflepuff colors, with his surname printed on the back of his torso, this Cedric minifigure is raring to go.

Dapper Diggory

The tournament isn't all hard work for the champions. Cedric Diggory scrubs up well for the Yule Ball. His minifigure has his usual swept-back hair piece and wears a very elegant black dinner jacket and tie with a dress shirt. Cheers!

Brick facts

The glittering Triwizard Cup is so momentous that it stands almost as tall as a minifigure, though it can still be held aloft with a single hand. It is one piece and has metallic printing around the rim.

Short, dark, textured hair piece

Durmstrang crest with double-headed eagle and stag's head

Valiant Viktor

Viktor's double-sided head can turn around to enjoy the Yule Ball festivities. Now smiling, he looks gallant in a red military-style jacket. Leather straps across his torso hold a fur-lined cape over one shoulder. His belt buckle has a miniature version of the Durmstrang crest.

Viktor Krum

The Goblet of Fire selects Viktor Krum from the Durmstrang Institute. He's met with great excitement at Hogwarts because he's already famous as the Seeker on the Bulgarian National Quidditch team. The Viktor minifigure has two expressions. His furrowed brow here suggests he is focused on outwitting his dragon, a Chinese Fireball.

Long hair tied up for challenge

Quilted tunic

Fleur's initials

Fancy Fleur

Fleur swaps her practical legs piece for an elegant sloped skirt brick for the Yule Ball. She wears an evening dress of silver-gray satin with leaf details. Fleur is so dazzling because her grandmother was a Veela—a semi-human, enchantingly beautiful creature.

Fleur Delacour

The brightest and the best from Beauxbatons Academy of Magic, Fleur Delacour is a very skilled witch, particularly with charms. Fleur defeats her Common Welsh Green dragon by enchanting it to sleep. Her minifigure wears a blue-and-gold tracksuit with a Beauxbatons crest on the back.

Beauxbatons' carriage

Hogwarts is hard to find on a map—there's no direct road to it, and you can't Apparate in its grounds either. Visitors often find their own clever ways to get there. Students from the Beauxbatons Academy of Magic make their appearance in style in a flying coach pulled by elegant, white, flying horses, when they arrive for the Triwizard Tournament.

A warm welcome

Groundskeeper Hagrid guides the carriage in to land. He greets the new guests and helps them unload their luggage. Hagrid also gives the horses a well-deserved drink from the bottle inside the trunk—they only drink single malt whiskey!

Fleur Delacour

Future Triwizard champion, Fleur arrives at Hogwarts in the carriage. She hasn't been selected for the tournament yet, so she wears her blue Beauxbatons uniform, like all her classmates. Fleur's hair and hat are a single piece and the other side of her double-printed head shows her singing.

Hair is tied back in a low ponytail

Medium-sized legs are molded in two shades of blue

Movable head with printed reins

Gabrielle Delacour

Fleur's little sister, Gabrielle, shares the same torso and hair piece as Fleur, but has shorter legs and freckles on her face. The other side of Gabrielle's head shows her sleeping. She is placed in an enchanted sleep at the bottom of the Great Lake to be rescued by Fleur as part of the tournament's second task.

Cape is printed on the front and back of torso

Madame Maxime

The half-giant Headmistress of Beauxbatons, Olympe Maxime, accompanies her students. Her minifigure is even taller than Hagrid's, thanks to a sloped skirt piece that is taller than regular sloped skirts by the height of one standard LEGO brick.

Fur collar

Extra-tall skirt piece is printed on the front and the back

Brick facts

After the journey, it's time for a cup of tea. This teapot piece also appears in other LEGO Harry Potter sets. Tina Goldstein uses one to rescue an Occamy and return it to Newt's case.

Windows slope outward

Lanterns can be removed and carried by minifigures

Ornate pearl-gold decorations

Set name
Beauxbatons' Carriage:
Arrival at Hogwarts
Year 2019
Set number 75958
Pieces 430
Minifigures 4

Short lattice fence piece is used on its side for a step

Front wheels rotate on a large turntable piece

Flying carriage

Beauxbatons' elegant powder-blue carriage is pulled by Madame Maxime's fine white Abraxans. These flying horses are very strong, which makes a journey in the carriage a wild ride. The carriage twists on a turntable behind the horses' harness.

Open house

Once safely on land, one side of the carriage folds up and over to create a two-story living space. Underneath there is room for relaxing and drinking tea. Upstairs are two beds and reading lights, two removable drawers, and a shelf.

Yule Ball

The Yule Ball is a tradition as old as the Triwizard Tournament itself. The ball celebrates international friendship between the three schools and gives the champions a break from the grueling tournament. On Christmas Eve night, everyone can dance their troubles away. Hogwarts Clock Tower set has been decorated as a winter wonderland for the festivities.

The Goblet of Fire

Triwizard champion Cedric Diggory enters the ball, passing the Goblet of Fire that burns with blue flames. The Goblet of Fire selects the students who compete in the Triwizard Tournament. Once chosen, they are bound by a magical contract and must take part.

Winter wonderland

Icicle-encrusted tables, sparkling glassware, and elegant ice sculptures adorn the busy ballroom. The buildable ice sculptures are made from transparent, pointed pieces. Minifigures of Dumbledore and Madame Maxime pause to chat, wearing their finest dress robes. Ron is talking to Fleur—perhaps he's asking her to dance?

Castle at Christmas

The festive Clock Tower set can be joined with other LEGO Hogwarts Castle sets to make a larger scene. It includes a three-story tower, the entrance hall, the Defense Against the Dark Arts classroom, the hospital wing with two beds, the prefects' bathroom, Dumbledore's office, and a star-topped Christmas tree.

Set name Hogwarts Clock Tower

Year 2019

Set number 75948

Pieces 922

Minifigures 8

Ron feels out of place in his unfashionable dress robes

Transparent ice sculpture

Icicle is a unicorn horn piece

Cones molded with roof-tile design

Brick facts

Hogwarts' clock has two separate dials. They are both radar dishes, printed with clock faces of Roman numerals. The smaller one is used elsewhere in a Winter Village Station set.

Inverse transparent radar dish for larger clock face

Revolving dance floor

The Ball is first and foremost a dance, and all the students have lessons beforehand. The champions open the dance, including Viktor Krum and his partner, Hermione. A revolving dance floor function really gets the minifigures moving by spinning them in two ways at once.

Snow-covered Christmas tree

Madame Maxime wears an elegant wrap dress

Lord Voldemort

Watch out! This spooky minifigure is Lord Voldemort—the vilest Dark wizard ever known. He was once a Hogwarts schoolboy called Tom Riddle, but now people are so afraid of him that they dare only call him He Who Must Not Be Named, or the Dark Lord. Voldemort craves power and will destroy anyone who stands in his way.

Wand to cast Dark curses and spells

Flat nose with snake-like nostrils

Green trim on black robes

Curved sloped brick for long, wizard robes

The Dark Lord

Voldemort was defeated many years ago, but not completely destroyed. A piece of his soul survived and waited years to regain a physical form. Now Voldemort has a body again, he's growing in strength and has had two LEGO minifigures produced. Both show his pale face with bloodshot eyes and a nose like a snake.

Heir of Slytherin

Like his distant ancestor Salazar Slytherin, Voldemort is a Parselmouth, which means he can talk to snakes. Fittingly, his companion in the LEGO Harry Potter Minifigure Series is a large snake named Nagini. Voldemort wears long Slytherin-green robes.

Bone-white skin

Nagini clips into Voldemort's hand

Tom Riddle

It's hard to believe, but long ago, Voldemort was a boy called Tom Riddle. He reappears as a boy after 50 years, emerging from his magical diary. He reopens the Chamber of Secrets and releases the Basilisk. Tom Riddle's exclusive LEGO minifigure is also found with a book—this one!

Old-fashioned Hogwarts uniform

Mold was used in 2016 for a minifigure baby in a tan blanket

Small, but dangerous

This small LEGO piece may look like a bizarre baby, but it is actually the Dark Lord! Reduced to just a fragment of his soul, Voldemort exists only as a tiny, writhing creature for many years. He has been plotting to get a proper body and finally he is close to achieving it.

Brick facts

A grave is stickered with the Deathly Hallows symbol. People say that the Elder Wand (the line), the Resurrection Stone (circle), and the Invisibility Cloak (triangle) can conquer death.

The rise of Voldemort

In this graveyard in Little Hangleton, Voldemort literally rises from beneath the ground with a new, physical body thanks to a LEGO flipping mechanism. A cauldron holds a potion that brings the Dark Lord back in a strong, human form. Held prisoner, Harry's minifigure can only watch on helplessly.

Gravestone reads "Tom Riddle"

Movable scythe holds Harry in place

Gray stone frog decorates gravestone

Cauldron with potion for bringing Voldemort back to full strength

Set name The Rise of Voldemort
Year 2019
Set number 75965
Pieces 184
Minifigures 5

Spinning section lifts Voldemort's figure out of the ground

Voldemort's followers

Voldemort is the most powerful wizard ever known, but even he can't do everything alone. He's dependent on an army of followers. They carry out his orders, sometimes due to loyalty and shared beliefs, but mostly out of plain fear. However, Voldemort gives no loyalty in return. He regards everyone as disposable when they are no longer useful.

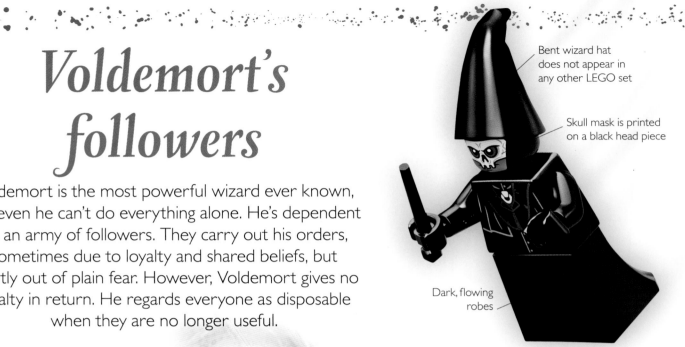

Bent wizard hat does not appear in any other LEGO set

Skull mask is printed on a black head piece

Dark, flowing robes

Death Eater

Voldemort's most loyal group of supporters are called Death Eaters. To protect their identities, they cover their faces with masks. This minifigure from The Rise of Voldemort (set 75965) could be anyone. The mystery individual answers their master's call to gather in a village graveyard for Voldemort's return.

Brick facts

Only Quirrell wears his turban in purple, but the piece has featured on two other minifigure heads. A Snake Charmer wears it in white and a Desert Warrior in dark green.

Bags under his eyes from physical strain and worry

Fabric from the turban is draped over his torso and shoulders

Quirinus Quirrell

In Harry's first year, Professor Quirrell teaches Defense Against the Dark Arts. Quirrell has traveled all over the world and adopted elements of the cultures that he has encountered, including a purple turban. He claims that an African prince gave it to him in return for saving him from a zombie.

Hapless host

Quirrell's minifigure reveals an appalling secret: he is sharing his body with Voldemort! Not only is Quirrell unable to defeat his own parasite, but he even brings it into Hogwarts. Hidden underneath Quirrell's lavender turban lies his master's withered, scowling face.

Rat-like features include furry eyebrows and large front teeth

Artificial hand (Pettigrew sacrificed his real one to Voldemort)

Peter Pettigrew

At school, Peter Pettigrew was a great friend of Sirius Black, Remus Lupin, and James Potter (Harry's father). However, he later betrayed them to Voldemort. Everyone thought he died a long time ago, but he has actually been in hiding. Pettigrew is a rat Animagus, which means he can transform into that animal at will.

Scabbers

If you smell a rat, it could be Ron's pet, Scabbers. Or it could be because there is deception here. Scabbers is actually the Animagus Peter Pettigrew, who has been biding his time in secret, living with the unknowing Weasley family.

Wild, curly hair

Stitched leather corset

Bellatrix Lestrange

Devoted to Lord Voldemort, Bellatrix is the Dark Lord's right-hand woman and an expert dueler. This menacing minifigure has no mercy and cackles with heartless glee at others' suffering. Proud to be called Voldemort's most faithful servant, she even sacrifices her own family for him.

Large eyes have no pupils

Scarred torso

Fenrir Greyback

If you're bitten by Fenrir Greyback, you don't turn into a LEGO minifigure—you turn into a werewolf! Fenrir is a vicious creature who relishes finding new victims. The creepy werewolf joins Voldemort's followers. He doesn't particularly support the Dark Lord, but selfishly wants to benefit from the chaos the Death Eaters create.

Fantastic Beasts

Newt Scamander

Born in 1897, Newton Artemis Fido Scamander turned his childhood passion for animals into a successful career as a Magizoologist. Newt has even written a book about the magical creatures he encounters—*Fantastic Beasts and Where to Find Them*. Newt's famous book becomes a core textbook at Hogwarts for many years to come.

Dapper 1920s-style suit and bow tie

Bowtruckle called Pickett lives in Newt's clothes

Animal lover

Newt's curiosity takes him around the world, studying creatures in their natural habitats. Scientists often treat their subjects coldly, but Newt really cares about all the creatures he studies. His minifigure can often be found with an animal companion.

Magical case accompanies Newt everywhere

Ruffled hairpiece is seen in a darker brown on Seamus Finnigan and Lucian Bole

Niffler clips onto minifigure's hand

Brick facts

This small LEGO® version of Newt's case can be carried by his minifigure (unlike the larger version, which he can walk around in). Thanks to a hinged side, the case can open and Newt can store items inside it.

Humble scientist

For such a celebrated Magizoologist (and accidental wizarding hero), Newt is very quiet and modest. He shuns the spotlight and is alarmed by many aspects of human life—like working in an office. Newt's happiest when he's with his beloved animals, such as his mischievous Niffler.

Surprising case

Newt wants to keep his animals safe, so he carries them everywhere in his battered leather case. It's much bigger on the inside, thanks to many extension charms. Newt's Case of Magical Creatures (set 75952) opens up to reveal multiple habitats, where all creatures can feel at home.

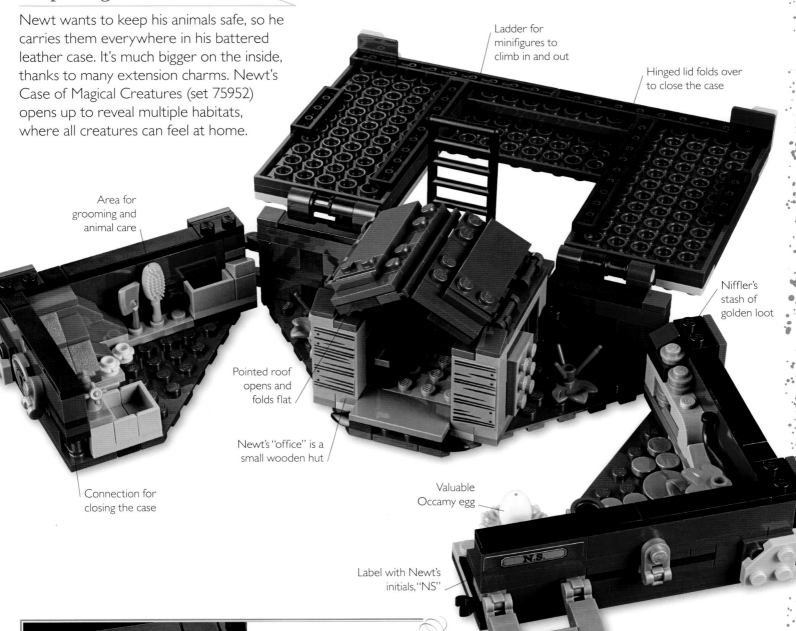

Ladder for minifigures to climb in and out

Hinged lid folds over to close the case

Area for grooming and animal care

Niffler's stash of golden loot

Pointed roof opens and folds flat

Newt's "office" is a small wooden hut

Connection for closing the case

Valuable Occamy egg

Label with Newt's initials, "NS"

Handle is covered with smooth tiles for easy carrying

Befriending Bowtruckles

Newt's respect for animals helps him win their trust. He has a special relationship with Bowtruckles—shy, twig-like creatures who guard wand-trees. Newt first met the species at school, where they ran away from everyone except him.

Set name Newt's Case of Magical Creatures

Year 2018

Set number 75952

Pieces 694

Minifigures 4

Fantastic beasts

Magizoologist Newt Scamander could tell you all about these magical creatures and where to find them—many of them are in his case! Whenever he comes across wild animals in need, he rescues them and nurtures them in his custom-built case until he can return them home. Others, like the Niffler, make friendly but somewhat pesky pets.

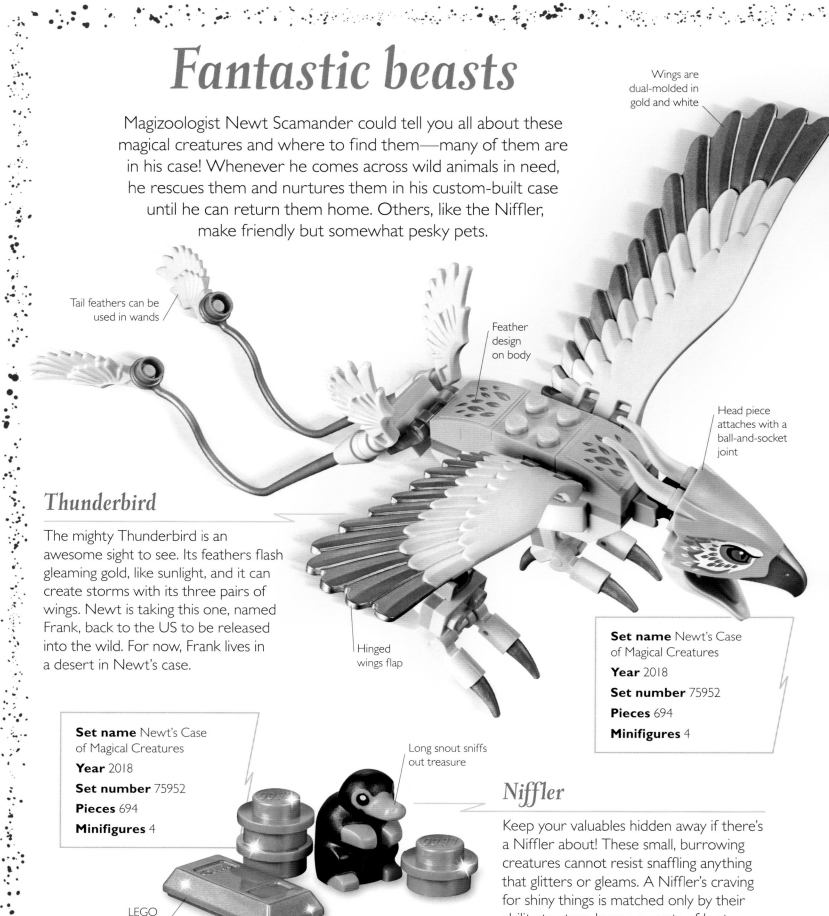

Wings are dual-molded in gold and white

Tail feathers can be used in wands

Feather design on body

Head piece attaches with a ball-and-socket joint

Thunderbird

The mighty Thunderbird is an awesome sight to see. Its feathers flash gleaming gold, like sunlight, and it can create storms with its three pairs of wings. Newt is taking this one, named Frank, back to the US to be released into the wild. For now, Frank lives in a desert in Newt's case.

Hinged wings flap

Set name Newt's Case of Magical Creatures

Year 2018

Set number 75952

Pieces 694

Minifigures 4

Set name Newt's Case of Magical Creatures

Year 2018

Set number 75952

Pieces 694

Minifigures 4

Long snout sniffs out treasure

LEGO ingot piece

Niffler

Keep your valuables hidden away if there's a Niffler about! These small, burrowing creatures cannot resist snaffling anything that glitters or gleams. A Niffler's craving for shiny things is matched only by their ability to store huge amounts of loot within a pouch in their tiny body.

Brick facts

The Occamy's head resembles a bird's and has the same LEGO mold as the Thunderbird. This head piece has two hinged pieces so the jaw opens and closes.

Occamy

Is it a bird? Is it a snake? The Occamy is a mixture of the two. It has a long, serpentine body, two wings, and an eagle-like head. An Occamy and one of its silvery-white eggs can be found in the LEGO version of Newt's Case. Be careful though—an Occamy can be vicious when protecting its nest!

Jointed body can be posed in different ways

Set name Newt's Case of Magical Creatures

Year 2018

Set number 75952

Pieces 694

Minifigures 4

Sturdy LEGO base so creature can stand up

Single mold for body, tail, and head

Eyes are printed to look like they glow

Set name Grindelwald's Escape

Year 2018

Set number 75951

Pieces 132

Minifigures 2

Dual-molded wings with transparent edges

Thestral

Skeletal Thestrals have a ghoulish reputation because they can only be seen by people who have witnessed death. They are actually very gentle creatures and can easily be domesticated. Thestrals are often used to pull carriages, like the one carrying Dark wizard Grindelwald during his bold escape from custody.

Bulky, brick-built body

Glowing Exploding Fluid

Erumpent

The bulky, rhino-like Erumpent is not normally violent, but when it is—watch out! Its large, sharp horn would be bad enough, but the real danger comes from the Exploding Fluid that it injects into anything it touches. Erumpents like open plains with water holes, including Muggle-filled Central Park in the center of New York City!

Horn is used in potions

Set name Newt's Case of Magical Creatures

Year 2018

Set number 75952

Pieces 694

Minifigures 4

77

Wizarding New York

English wizard Newt Scamander travels to America in 1926. He has rescued a stolen Thunderbird, which he wants to take back to its home in Arizona. However, passing through New York City on the way, Newt finds himself entangled with many new people. He quickly discovers that life in New York isn't as straightforward as he imagined.

Anti-witchcraft propaganda material

Percival Graves

Percival Graves is an important wizard in American law enforcement, but his body has been hijacked by the Dark wizard Grindelwald. This minifigure comes with a second hair piece and the other side of its head has Grindelwald's white moustache and eyebrows, showing his true form emerging.

Gray-and-black dual-molded hair piece

Tidy suit

Rare arm printing

Grindelwald's true white hair

Credence Barebone

Poor Credence doesn't know who he really is. He keeps his magical ability hidden because his adopted mother campaigns against witchcraft. But suppressing magic comes at a cost: Credence develops a Dark power called an Obscurus, which he cannot control. The reverse of his dual-sided head shows his eyes when the Obscurus takes over his body.

1920s-style hat is molded to hair piece

Sausage clips into bun

Tina Goldstein

Porpentina Goldstein, known as Tina, is a talented Auror who works for MACUSA (the Magical Congress of the United States of America). Tina is eating a hot dog when she first sees Newt, so her minifigure also carries this popular New York snack.

Tina to the rescue

In Newt's Case of Magical Creatures (set 75952), Tina has taken off her hat and overcoat. She holds a teapot with a removable lid, in which she captured the Occamy that was on the loose in New York. Now Tina returns the half-bird, half-snake creature to the safety of Newt's suitcase.

Fruit strudel is made in moments with Queenie's wand

Decorative roses made from apple slices

Tickled pink

Queenie loves to cook for people, and in Newt's Case of Magical Creatures (set 75952) she beams as she feeds the giant Thunderbird. This version of Queenie wears a long coat with a wide collar in shades of pink. Her alternate face print looks more alarmed.

Queenie Goldstein

Lively and friendly Queenie is Tina's younger sister. The sisters live together in a New York apartment and both work for MACUSA. Queenie is a Legilimens, which means she can read people's thoughts and feelings. Her minifigure wears a blue, sailor-inspired dress and has soft, blonde curls cut short in a 1920s style.

Seraphina Picquery

Madam Seraphina Picquery is President of MACUSA. She faces the biggest disaster of her career in Grindelwald's Escape (set 75951), when transporting the world's most dangerous prisoner goes terribly wrong. Hopefully a wave of her unique purple wand can save the day!

Hat is unique to this minifigure

Blonde hair curl

Bright magenta lipstick

Erumpent target

Jacob wears a leather vest to protect him from a rampaging Erumpent. He also has a helmet to swap for his hair. The helmet goes with his alternate face printing, which features a chinstrap. Unlucky Jacob is armed only with a Bowtruckle and an umbrella!

Jacob Kowalski

An honest New Yorker, Jacob is a Muggle (or No-Maj, as the Americans say) who dreams of opening his own bakery. In the Minifigure Series, he carries a case with tasty treats that he hopes will tempt a bank manager into giving him a business loan.

Baked goodies

Grindelwald's carriage

In the 1920s, the Dark wizard Grindelwald was captured by the Magical Congress of the United States of America (MACUSA). However, someone so powerful is hard to contain—and even harder to move between prisons. Grindelwald is such a high-profile, dangerous prisoner that his journey is overseen by the MACUSA President, Seraphina Picquery, herself.

Brick facts

The transparent blue power blast piece was first developed for LEGO sets containing super heroes. Here, it can be launched out of a minifigure's hands to replicate a shooting spell.

Power blast piece

LEGO plant piece used in black for the first time

Roof section removes easily for playing

Seraphina Picquery does her best to duel with Grindelwald

Large spoked wheel appears in black for the first time in this set

Step for minifigures to climb into coach

Classic carriage

Based on a 1920s horse-drawn carriage, this elegant stagecoach is the scene of Grindelwald's bold escape from MACUSA custody. It's pulled by a flying Thestral and has an open-air seat for the driver. The passengers inside sit on plush red velvet seats—until Grindelwald decides to break out!

Front section steers differently from the back wheels

Entrance and exits

Both sides of the carriage feature opening doors for dual access. The carriage roof also removes easily to allow minifigures to be placed inside. Perhaps a vehicle carrying such a dangerous prisoner shouldn't have so many methods of getting out!

Gellert Grindelwald

One pale gray eye

The Dark wizard Grindelwald wants a world where witches and wizards rule over Muggles, and he'll destroy anyone to achieve it. His minifigure shows him as he really is—without any Polyjuice Potion or spells. But don't provoke him or he could reveal the scary side of his head.

Necklace chain under an open-necked collar

Neat, double-breasted waistcoat

Wings molded from solid and transparent black plastic

Escape to Europe

MACUSA's plan to was transport Grindelwald from an American prison to Europe so he could stand trial for crimes he committed there. However, Grindelwald claims the carriage for himself. He's now free to continue building his army of followers.

Bony neck

Bars are connected to removable plates built into the Thestral's body

Set name Grindelwald's Escape

Year 2018

Set number 75951

Pieces 132

Minifigures 2

Behind the Scenes

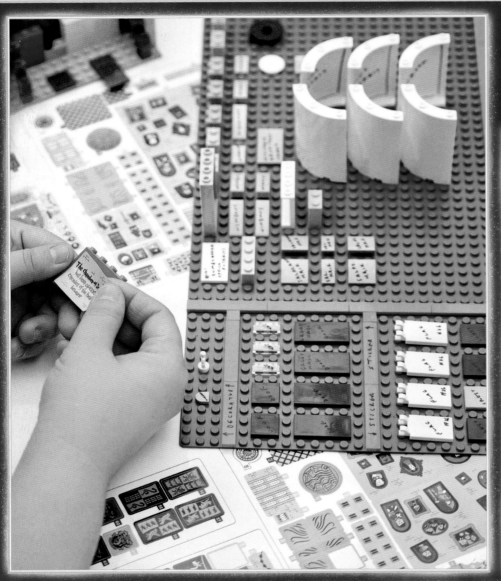

Meet the team

The LEGO Group returned to the Wizarding World in 2018 for a new range of LEGO® Harry Potter™ sets, plus models and minifigures based on the *Fantastic Beasts* movies. The LEGO Harry Potter team went on to win two coveted Toy of the Year Awards in 2019. Here, the team gives us a peek behind-the-scenes in Billund, Denmark, and reveal how they work their magic to create such spellbinding sets.

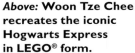

Above: **Woon Tze Chee recreates the iconic Hogwarts Express in LEGO® form.**

Left: **Model designers Marcos Bessa and James Stephenson discuss The Knight Bus (set 75957). The challenge on this set was to create a curved roof, which windows could be attached to securely.**

There are so many iconic moments from the Harry Potter films. How do you decide which ones to recreate in LEGO sets?

Marcos Bessa There's certainly a huge amount to draw inspiration from, so choosing which moments to translate into LEGO sets isn't an easy task! Often, we start by talking to Warner Bros. about their upcoming plans for the Wizarding World. We also think about who we are building the sets for and how much they know about LEGO bricks and Harry's world. This helps us decide how recognizable (or obscure!) our models, minifigures, and references can be.

Mark Stafford The first thing I did was sit down with a pad and write down what key locations I remembered from each movie and book. It had been several years since I had seen or read any of them, so this gave me a list of truly memorable rooms and buildings to consider recreating in the "sketch models" I made next.

Once you've decided what the set will be, how do you begin building?

Woon Tze Chee Re-watching the movies is a good way to start. We pay attention to every detail of the subject matter and identify what special functions, details, or surprises we could include in the sets. Some designers prefer sketching out ideas on paper first, while others might jump right into building with bricks. We all seek feedback from others involved in the project to improve the model.

Mark Before we started the 2018 products, we also spent a day at the Warner Bros. Studio Tour in the UK. I took more than 300 photographs of weird and wonderful details. The inside of Dumbledore's cupboards, Diagon Alley shop windows, the Hogwarts Express sweet trolley, the model of the Great Hall's roof, statues ... On top of the research we normally do to create LEGO sets, this was a really special experience and helped a huge amount.

The Harry Potter characters are so beloved, how do you go about recreating them in minifigure form?

Austin Carlson First, we created a library of photos taken at the Warner Bros. Studio Tour of props and outfits that the characters actually used and wore in the films. Then we collected a lot of images from the films to add to our library of reference. But what really helped out was being a fan!

Lorraine Faure It is fun to look at the characters' iconic outfits and find the best way to translate them into minifigures. I'm always wondering what's the best feature to pick and how to simplify it to make it work at a minifigure scale. Take Professor Slughorn in Hogwarts Astronomy Tower (set 75969)—it was very interesting to find the right balance between the heavy pattern of his outfit and the cool details: his watch chain, pompoms, and bow tie.

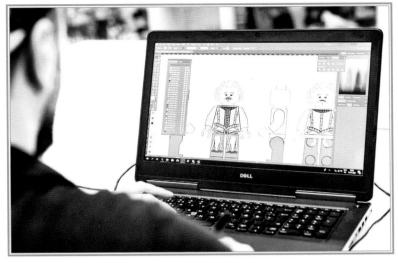

Final character designs are considered from every angle, including **Nearly Headless Nick's double-sided (and famously removable) head piece.**

Which is your favorite LEGO Harry Potter minifigure?

Austin Luna! One of my favorite characters but one of the most fun to design as well!

Casper Glahder I always enjoyed working on the darker, more edgy characters. So I was really happy to work on Sirius Black. He is one of my favorite characters in the movies and it was fun to try and make a minifigure of him. He has escaped after many years of imprisonment, so he needed to look like he was in a rough state. I was also very happy to work on Fenrir Greyback. It is always fun to try and make something as cute as a minifigure look scary.

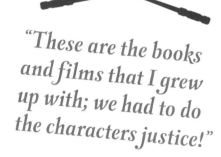

"These are the books and films that I grew up with; we had to do the characters justice!"

Austin Carlson

How did you decide on the Tom Riddle minifigure for this book?

Marcos When the challenge was to create an exclusive figure for an in-depth book of the LEGO Harry Potter universe, it became clear to us that we should go for something a bit deeper into the story that true Harry Potter fans would recognize and appreciate. Tom Riddle is—SPOILER ALERT!—none other than "He Who Must Not Be Named" before he became Lord Voldemort. Offering this very special version of the character with this book was an opportunity that we did not want to pass on.

Djordje Djordjevic and Crystal Fontan review minifigure designs, which are based on reference material from the movies and visits to Warner Bros. Studio Tour.

Which was the most challenging set to create?

Samuel Johnson I worked on Newt's Case of Magical Creatures (set 75952). The concept was to make a little case become something big for maximum play opportunities. It was rather challenging to add a building for Newt, as well as environments for each of the Fantastic Beasts that are included in the set.

Wesley Talbott Hedwig (set 75979) was definitely the most challenging. We have very high standards to ensure stability in our models. Making the flapping function required a lot of trial and error to make sure the model would stay together after lots of play.

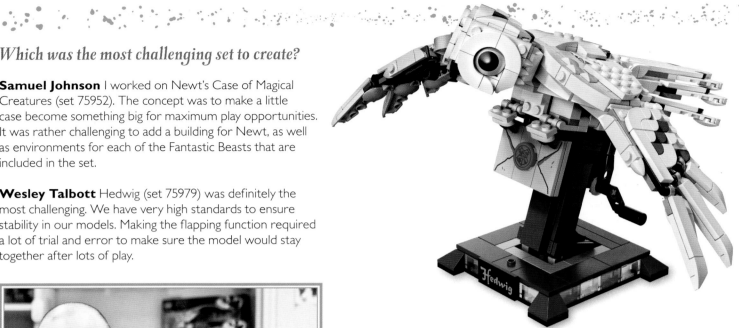

Wesley Talbott experiments with the functionality of Hedwig (set 75979) to ensure the wings work.

Some sets combine to create a larger Hogwarts build. How are interconnected sets like these developed by the team?

Mark Early on, I came up with the idea to make a modular version of Hogwarts. The "sketch model" I built was very big! It featured the Great Hall and the Clock Tower entrance as the two largest modules, as well as classrooms, the Gryffindor common room, kitchens, bridge, and walls. The idea was almost dropped later in development, until Raphaël realized the Hogwarts build in his Whomping Willow set would fit really nicely on the side of my Great Hall set. With minor changes to both of our models, the modular idea was resurrected! I put a connection point on the other side of the Hall, too, so when Woon Tze was later asked to develop my Clock Tower entrance into a set, we could connect it in a similar way to the original modular sketch models.

Hogwarts Clock Tower (set 75948), Hogwarts Great Hall (set 75954), Hogwarts Whomping Willow (set 75953), and Hogwarts Astronomy Tower (set 75969) connect to make one big scene.

Hogwarts Castle (set 71043) is the second biggest LEGO set ever made! What goes into making a set like this?

Justin Ramsden Obviously we knew that Hogwarts Castle is a huge location to recreate in LEGO form, but until we started constructing it physically, we didn't know that it would be this big! This was a doubly challenging set as it was designed to be microscale—a LEGO building style in which models are constructed smaller than in standard minifigure scale. Representing key architectural structures, iconic silhouettes, and other details in tiny bricks, while retaining the unforgettable look and feel of the films, was not an easy task.

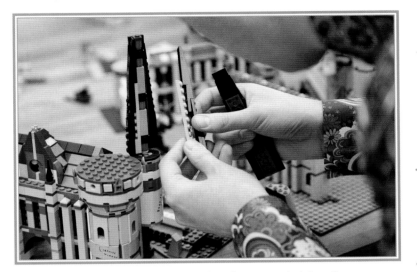

During the early stages of model development, bricks of different colors are used, depending on what is close at hand.

Crystal Fontan tests sticker prototypes for the set's 63 different sticker designs.

"My design approach to this set mainly focused on capturing the essence of Hogwarts: its iconic silhouette, the exciting feeling of going back to school, and ultimately starting a new adventure."

Justin Ramsden

Justin (continued) Once I was happy with the set's exterior, I began choosing the specific rooms that would fill the interior. These were selected due to their prominence in the Harry Potter stories, but also how recognizable they would be at such a small scale. An amazing team of LEGO Graphic Designers (run by the brilliant Crystal Fontan) brought in an additional layer of magic and storytelling. Their illustrations and stickers depict icons and locations that bricks at that tiny size just couldn't capture.

One detail that LEGO fans may not have noticed is that the piece count of the model is 6,020 LEGO elements. I landed on this amount of LEGO parts by chance. However, this number is significant for me because it is the set number of a classic LEGO castle model that I had when I was five years old, which coincidentally featured a wizard. This was one of the sets that inspired me to become a LEGO designer!

Which is your favorite set in the LEGO Harry Potter range?

James Stephenson I am a fan of sets with a big reveal. I enjoy the great open-and-close function in Newt's case. I also love brick-built creatures and the ones included in the case are awesome! Beauxbatons' Carriage: Arrival at Hogwarts (set 75958) is another favorite. I really liked it in the movie and it was great to finally see it appear in a LEGO collection.

Justin I really love the design of Hagrid's Hut: Buckbeak's Rescue (set 75947). Not only is this one of my favorite buildings from the Wizarding World, creating this interesting structure out of predominantly square LEGO parts isn't an easy task! I feel that Raphaël, the designer of the model, has managed to capture the shape of the building really well. The set also has a light-brick function and lots of storytelling elements crammed in, too—ten points to Gryffindor!

What new parts were introduced for the LEGO Harry Potter theme?

Austin One of the biggest additions to the Wizarding World and also the minifigure world is medium-sized legs. With the addition of the new leg size, we were able to fully show how the kids aged throughout their time at Hogwarts. We also brought the magic more to life by introducing new wand elements!

Tara Wike Some of the new elements we introduced in the Collectible Minifigure Series were a new sculpted head for Dobby, a megaphone for Professor Flitwick, a strudel for Queenie Goldstein, a cute little Niffler, a Mandrake plant, plus many new hair pieces!

Which is your favorite of all the creatures and beasts featured in the theme?

James Hands down, the Thunderbird from Newt's case. Crystal did an amazing job on head decoration for this (and for the Occamy) and the build itself is really cool. I also love the inclusion of the golden-tipped wings. It makes the overall appearance something really special.

Samuel When I visited Warner Bros. Studio Tours in London, I was really excited by the dark forest and the scary Aragog that they had there! It was great fun to design. Spiders are my favorite thing to build out of LEGO bricks!

Crystal Fontan compares the digital design of the Occamy head to the final printing (right), alongside Casper Glahder and Djordje Djordjevic.

"My favorite creatures are the Thunderbird, Occamy, and Hungarian Horntail, because even though they all use the same head element, they all look different! It was quite a challenge and I think I succeeded!"

Crystal Fontan

What mechanisms or movable LEGO pieces have you used to recreate a magical spell or enchantment?

Marcos It wasn't to create a magical spell or enchantment, but I was very happy when I succeeded in building the opening function of the Beauxbatons' Carriage. Having access to the inside of the model in an unexpected way, which also enhances the playability of the model, is—in itself—kinda magic! Does that count?

James For the Quidditch Match (set 75956), we wanted to give the impression of some minifigures in flight. While the function is simple, using the transparent pole element allowed us to make Oliver Wood fly backward and forward in front of the goal posts. It adds a touch of magic and a game playing layer to the set.

An early prototype or "sketch model" of Quidditch Match featuring the flying mechanism.

What's the best thing about working on the magical LEGO Harry Potter theme?

Marcos I played with some of the first LEGO Harry Potter products in the early 2000s, so being part of the team responsible for revisiting that universe is a dream come true. I grew up with Harry Potter and the LEGO sets allowed me to bring home some of that magic I had read about in the books or seen on the big screen. Now, our team has the opportunity to elevate those memories we share and create even better products that will inspire and delight kids of all ages, the same way I was inspired when building with my own LEGO sets as a kid.

Mark The fans' reaction has been incredible. So many years of pent-up LEGO Harry Potter anticipation was released, and the reaction was great. The fans have been so appreciative of everything we do and spot every single piece of obscure Potter trivia we include in the models. It's amazing.

Wesley The best part about designing Harry Potter models is exploring the reference material, studying the movie sets, and trying to translate as many small details as possible into LEGO bricks. I also love listening to the audio books while I work.

Justin As a child, I used to line up at the bookstore for the release of the new Harry Potter books. I was in awe of the adventures that Harry and his friends went on, and wrote a letter to the LEGO Group asking them to produce LEGO Harry Potter sets so that I could play out these brilliant stories in brick form. Now, over 20 years later, I'm lucky enough to create models based on a franchise that I still love and that fans all over the world line up to get their hands on. This is still jaw-dropping and I'm very very lucky to work on this magical theme!

"Working on this theme you get to appreciate how expansive and rich the Wizarding World is. Everything from the characters, scenes, and story lines offers a rich catalog of inspiration for us to work from and replicate in our models and minifigures."

James Stephenson

Some members of the LEGO Harry Potter team pictured in the LEGO Group headquarters in Billund, Denmark.

(left to right, top to bottom: Esa Nousiainen; Casper Glahder; Woon Tze Chee; Crystal Fontan; Tara Wike; Jakob Nielsen; Andrew Seenan; James Stephenson; Mark Stafford; Wesley Talbott; Raphaël Pretesacque; Justin Ramsden; Marcos Bessa; Austin Carlson; Joel Baker; Samuel Johnson.)

Character gallery

LEGO® minifigures are made out of three basic sections: the hips and legs, the torso (with arms and hands), and the head. This magical array of LEGO® Harry Potter™ and LEGO® Fantastic Beasts™ minifigures feature many incredible molds and accessories, including unique hair pieces, hats, wands, owls, brooms, and cloaks—even an Invisibility Cloak!

Harry Potter
(2018)

Harry Potter
(2018)

Harry Potter
(2018)

Harry Potter
(2018)

Harry Potter
(2019)

Harry Potter
(2018)

Harry Potter
(2020)

Harry Potter
(2019)

Harry Potter
(2018)

Harry Potter
(2019)

Harry Potter
(2019)

Harry Potter
(2019)

Harry Potter
(2020)

Harry Potter
(2020)

Harry Potter
(2020)

Ron Weasley
(2018)

Ron Weasley
(2018)

Ron Weasley
(2018)

Ron Weasley
(2018)

Ron Weasley
(2019)

Ron Weasley
(2018)

Ron Weasley
(2019)

Ron Weasley
(2020)

Ron Weasley
(2020)

Hermione Granger
(2018)

Hermione Granger
(2019)

Hermione Granger
(2018)

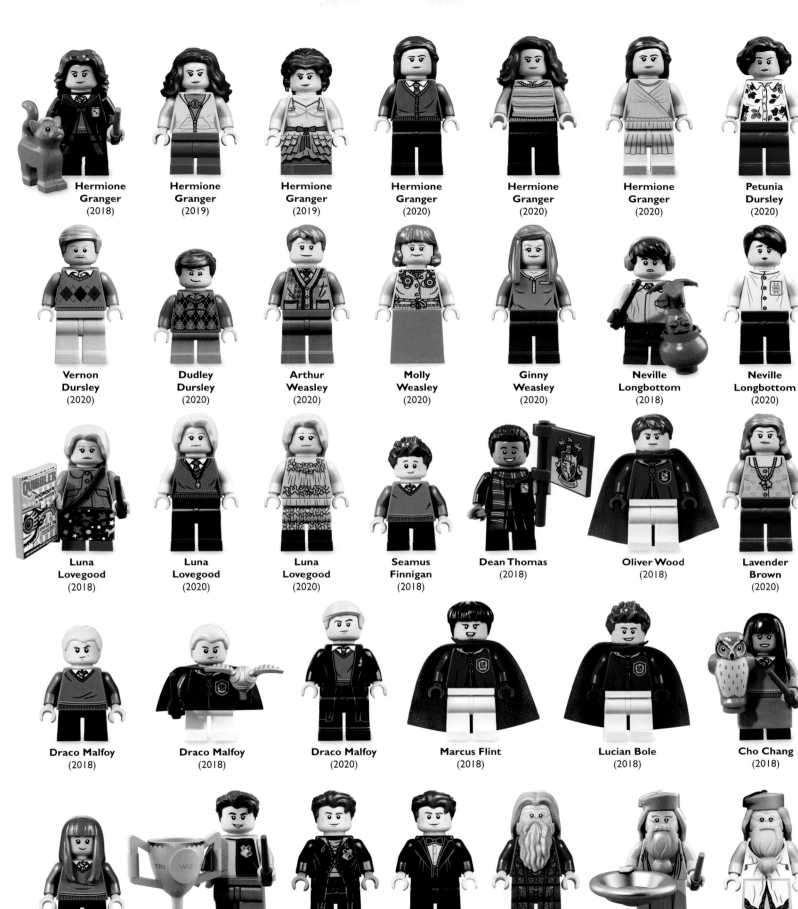

Hermione Granger (2018)

Hermione Granger (2019)

Hermione Granger (2019)

Hermione Granger (2020)

Hermione Granger (2020)

Hermione Granger (2020)

Petunia Dursley (2020)

Vernon Dursley (2020)

Dudley Dursley (2020)

Arthur Weasley (2020)

Molly Weasley (2020)

Ginny Weasley (2020)

Neville Longbottom (2018)

Neville Longbottom (2020)

Luna Lovegood (2018)

Luna Lovegood (2020)

Luna Lovegood (2020)

Seamus Finnigan (2018)

Dean Thomas (2018)

Oliver Wood (2018)

Lavender Brown (2020)

Draco Malfoy (2018)

Draco Malfoy (2018)

Draco Malfoy (2020)

Marcus Flint (2018)

Lucian Bole (2018)

Cho Chang (2018)

Susan Bones (2018)

Cedric Diggory (2018)

Cedric Diggory (2019)

Cedric Diggory (2019)

Professor Dumbledore (2018)

Professor Dumbledore (2018)

Professor Dumbledore (2019)

Professor McGonagall (2018)

Professor Snape (2018)

Boggart imitating Snape (2018)

Professor Flitwick (2018)

Professor Flitwick (2019)

Hagrid (2018)

Hagrid (2019)

Madam Hooch (2018)

Professor Trelawney (2018)

Professor Umbridge (2018)

Professor Umbridge (2020)

Professor Slughorn (2018)

Professor Slughorn (2020)

Argus Filch (2018)

Nearly Headless Nick (2018)

Godric Gryffindor (2018)

Salazar Slytherin (2018)

Rowena Ravenclaw (2018)

Helga Hufflepuff (2018)

Mr. Ollivander (2018)

Trolley Witch (2018)

Dobby (2018)

Dobby (2020)

Stan Shunpike (2019)

Ernie Prang (2019)

Cornelius Fudge (2019)

The Executioner (2019)

Dementor (2018)

Sirius Black (2019)

Remus Lupin (2018)

"Mad-Eye" Moody (2018)

Nymphadora Tonks (2020)

Fleur Delacour (2019)

Fleur Delacour (2019)

Fleur Delacour (2019)

Gabrielle Delacour (2019)

Madame Maxime (2019)

Madame Maxime (2019)

Viktor Krum (2019)

Viktor Krum (2019)

Lord Voldemort (2018)

Lord Voldemort (2019)

Tom Riddle (2020)

Lord Voldemort (2019)

Professor Quirrell (2018)

Peter Pettigrew (2019)

Death Eater (2019)

Fenrir Greyback (2020)

Bellatrix Lestrange (2020)

Fantastic Beasts

Newt Scamander (2018)

Newt Scamander (2018)

Tina Goldstein (2018)

Tina Goldstein (2018)

Jacob Kowalski (2018)

Jacob Kowalski (2018)

Queenie Goldstein (2018)

Queenie Goldstein (2018)

Percival Graves (2018)

Credence Barebone (2018)

Seraphina Picquery (2018)

Gellert Grindelwald (2018)

Index

Main entries are highlighted in **bold**.
Sets are listed by their full name.

DK | Penguin Random House

Project Editor Beth Davies
Project Art Editor Jenny Edwards
Editors Ruth Amos, Matt Jones
Designers Lisa Sodeau, Stefan Georgiou
Production Editor Siu Yin Chan
Senior Producer Lloyd Robertson
Managing Editor Paula Regan
Managing Art Editor Jo Connor
Publisher Julie Ferris
Art Director Lisa Lanzarini
Publishing Director Mark Searle

First American Edition, 2020
Published in the United States by DK Publishing
1450 Broadway, Suite 801, New York, NY 10018

Page design copyright © 2020 Dorling Kindersley Limited
DK, a Division of Penguin Random House LLC
20 21 22 23 24 10 9 8 7 6 5 4 3 2 1
001–316404–July/2020

Anglia is a trademark owned and licensed by Ford Motor Company.

A catalog record for this book
is available from the Library of Congress.
ISBN: 978-1-4654-9237-1
ISBN: 978-1-4654-9612-6 (library edition)

Printed in China

For the curious

www.dk.com
www.LEGO.com

Slytherin
spectator tower

Gryffindor
spectator tower

Acknowledgments

Dorling Kindersley would like to thank: Gary
Ombler for minifigure photography, Nicole
Reynolds for editorial assistance, Julia March
for proofreading and the index, and Megan
Douglass for Americanization.
The publishers would also like to thank: Randi
Sørensen, Heidi K. Jensen, Paul Hansford,
Martin Leighton Lindhardt, Marcos Bessa,
Helene Desprets, and Stine Mosgaard at the
LEGO Group; Victoria Selover and Katie
Campbell at Warner Bros., and Natalie
Laverick from The Blair Partnership.
Thanks to Thomas Baunsgaard for behind-
the-scenes photography.

For the behind-the-scenes chapter, thanks to
members of the LEGO Harry Potter team
(2018–2020): Andrew Hugh Seenan, Tara
Wike, Marcos Bessa, Michael Vibede Vantin,
Helene Desprets, Stine Mosgaard Jensen,
Stine Bagge, Charlotte Fey, Michael Albæk,
Dorte Knudsen Munk, Patricia Vaiaóga Voulund
Andersen, Samuel Thomas Liltorp Johnson,
Justin Ramsden, Raphaël Pierre Roger
Pretesacque, Mark John Stafford, James
Stephenson, Marcos Bessa, Luis F. E. Castaneda,
Woon Tze Chee, Wesley Alan Talbott, Austin
William Carlson, Crystal Marie Fontan, Djordje
Djordjevic, Casper Glahder, Lorraine Faure,
Esa Nousiainen, Jakob Nielsen.